CHAMPION OF
CHAMPIONS

CHAMPION OF CHAMPIONS

David Brayley

Scratching Shed Fiction

A catalogue record for this book is available from the British
Library.

Typeset in Iowan Old Style Bold and Times New Roman
Printed and bound in the United Kingdom by
Ashford Colour Press
Fareham Road, Gosport, Hampshire.

"This is a great, inspirational and pacy read, beautifully written and utterly enriching with a stunning climax..."
– Peter James

Foreword

Peter James
International best-selling thriller writer

❋

THIS terrific book contains two things that are dear to my heart. The love of sport and the love of reading. Although written principally for the young adult market, I think this is a book that would appeal to all ages, regardless of whether you love cycling or not.

It is a deep, rich story about family conflict, history, determination, achievement and ultimate success. I hope you enjoy it.

It fully deserves a wide readership.

Peter James,
Sussex, 2017

To Andrea Carrea. Cyclist.

August 14 1924 – January 13 2013

His story inspired this book.

Introduction
Milan, Italy. Spring 2017

'PAIN is temporary. It may last a minute, or an hour, or a day, or a year, but eventually it will subside and something else will take its place. If I quit, however, it lasts forever...' – Lance Armstrong.

Interesting quote that.

My name is Daniel Williams and I first read that statement when I was twenty, back in 2008, when I still believed every word that my then hero, Lance Armstrong said. Despite the fact that I now know that Armstrong was living a lie, the quote itself remains relevant and I wish I could have read it when I was thirteen, at a time when I used to quit for fun. I was always pretty good at sport in school, quite talented really, but when the going got tough, well, put it this way, I never really got going.

One occasion that haunts me still is when we had a school sports day at my comprehensive school in Bishopston on the Gower and I was picked to represent my House, Talbot, in the 400 metres. I knew

I wouldn't win, that was always the domain of Chris Lewis who never lost a race in the five years we were there, but I was easily good enough to come second. I realised this when I was told that most of my regular opponents from previous years – good runners too – were running in the 200 or 800 metres instead, so wouldn't be in my race. Long before the gun went off, I knew I was going to do well. Very well.

I stood on the start line doing some stretches, waiting for the start, smiling at some of the girls in the crowd and basically going through the motions. I was supremely confident and was actually more concerned with looking good than worrying too much about the inevitable second place and eight house points I was about to win.

Out of the corner of my eye, I saw two of my new competitors who were running instead of the more talented guys, Robert Edwards and Martin Stephens – the replacements. 'Replacements' was one word for them I suppose, but I had another – losers. They were nice enough lads, but not in my league in terms of sporting ability. Neither had played football, rugby or cricket for the school like I had, I viewed them as imposters, imposters who had no place lining up next to the likes of me. I was super confident, second place was going to be a walk in the park.

Our PE teacher, Mr Harries, fired his gun and off we went. As usual, Chris Lewis was ten metres ahead by the time the rest of us had run the first bend to begin the second hundred meters. I was clicking along nicely and as we reached the top of the back straight, with just over 200 to go, I was running totally effortlessly and within myself, just waiting for the pats on the back and smiles from the girls I'd be receiving after I'd rolled in for that all important second place and those precious eight points it would bring Talbot House.

Then the roars began.

I glanced to my left, and there, on the two inside lanes were the losers, Robert and Martin. Only thing was, they weren't running anything like losers. I decided it was time for me to put these upstarts in their place once and for all, so picked up my pace for the last 150 to shake them off.

It didn't work.

As we entered the last 100, panic. The three of us were in a line, and I was flat out, I'd hit my maximum pace. I glanced left for a split second and saw the determination on the faces of the losers. I tried to kick for the last time. And as I did Robert edged past me.

Two strides later so did Martin.

For about four strides I just about kept up with them both, then time stopped still for me and a horrific realisation quickly hit me right between the eyes. I could see up ahead that Chris had already won, but I could also see all the faces lining the finishing straight, laughing at me whilst witnessing the process of me being beaten by a pair of losers! I could also see something else too, and that was the humiliation I was going to get from my mates, with all their mickey taking over the coming weeks, every time Robert and Martin walked past me in the yard. I was also facing the predictable disappointment of my PE teacher, Mr Harries, explaining that once again, my laziness had 'Let yourself, and everybody else in your House, down.'

Time started again, and I realised that I still had about thirty metres to run; I could still do it! I instantly snapped myself out of my self-imposed trance and tried as hard as I could to reduce the now two metre gap between me and the losers. In a couple of determined strides, I actually got back level with Robert, but was still a further stride down on Martin, but I was struggling. My legs were bursting with lactic acid and were murdering me with the pain, my lungs were on fire and my stomach was being turned inside out to the point of vomit. I was tasting unbelievable pain, but far worse than that, also facing painful humiliation. But, deep inside, I knew that if I stuck in there, I could still beat them and save face.

If I stuck in there.

Fifteen metres to go, the three of us were back level.

Twelve metres to go, Martin edged back ahead.

Ten metres to go, so did Robert.

Eight metres to go, I quit. I almost came to a stop immediately once I'd made the decision to give up, my legs instantly becoming jelly like, making me wobble like a drunk on his way back from the pub. I tried to pretend it was all a joke and that I'd let the boys beat me, but as I jogged to the line, trying desperately to look cool and as if none of this bothered me, more cheers from the crowd as Ian Thomas, a prop forward from our rugby team, lunged and dipped at the line to edge me out to fifth place. A prop! My humiliation was complete. I didn't know where to look, and the laughter and finger pointing burned right to the very heart of my soul.

Within two minutes of the end of the race, and wallowing in a sea of self-pity having had to accept the humiliation and mocking laughter from just about everyone who was there, I was completely recovered physically. All the pain had disappeared and I was feeling as though I could actually run the whole thing again. There were so many of my mates laughing at me, that a re-run seemed the only option, but I knew it was never going to happen. The awful realisation had hit me that when the key moment of the race came, in that last fifteen metres or so, I'd been faced with the choice to dig deep and give everything, or quit. And I'd chosen to quit. Amongst all the mocking and ridicule, I knew that I'd have to live with being exposed publically as a quitter, along with the shame it brought ... for ever.

And I have. To this very day that race still haunts me.

It's been an extremely long road from that school sports day, all those years ago, to here, my hotel room in Northern Italy, awaiting the most important bike race of my career which takes place tomorrow morning. But it's no longer a school four hundred metre race that will test my staying power and commitment; it's something far bigger than that. I've been a professional road cyclist for the past six years since I was initially signed on by the Belgian team Cyclo-Kas-Power as a promising twenty two year old after a glittering youth career, and four years in the British Olympic Track cycling squad. However, I had my fair share of injuries when I tried – and failed – to make the final 2012 Olympic squad, and been released by plenty of pro teams since then too, so tomorrow morning, as I take to the start of the legendary Milan – San Remo race on the streets of the fashion city as a totally unknown outsider, it's not just a race that's at stake ... it's my whole career. My team manager at my current team, MotoStep, Jacques Deschamps, has just left my room and told me that tomorrow will be my last race with them unless I do something special. No pressure then ... the stakes couldn't be higher.

But, do you know what? That's fine by me. Why? Because I'm a changed man. I no longer quit.

You see, I now understand Lance Armstrong's 'quitting' quote more deeply and intensely than you'll ever probably know. Despite most things that Armstrong said during his career now appearing to be tainted by his awful lies, his quote still holds massive importance for me. Quite simply, quitting is not an option for me any longer – it really is as simple as that. And quitting certainly isn't part of the plan that I have in mind for tomorrow's contest. Whatever happens tomorrow, I'm even prepared to die on my bike. I will not quit. I simply won't allow that to happen.

You are probably thinking that I learned the importance of never giving up after that humiliating defeat in the school sports day 400 metres, and I'd love to say that was the case, but I quit many, many more times after that. For a while following that black day, I still blamed everyone and anything I could think of for the defeat, instead of the real culprit – me. I needed far more than losing a race in the worst possible way to remove the lazy streak as wide as a mile that lay deep within me. But then, I got lucky, very lucky. I stumbled across inspiration and direction from a man who had never known the meaning of the word quit in his life. Someone who would teach me about not just how a person should never, ever give up, but also by introducing me to and instructing me in, the single most important lesson any young person could ever learn in life:

Be the best that you can be.

This man showed me that if a person can be the best they can be in any walk of life – sport or otherwise – then they will realise and discover that they will have an excellent chance of succeeding at anything. In addition to his wise advice, this man also helped convince me that I could one day make it into the ranks of elite sport. He achieved this largely thanks to his inspirational storytelling to me of the life of one of the greatest cyclists of all time who was ultimately to become my unlikely spiritual guide. You won't have heard of this cyclist yet, but his nickname tells you all you really need to know about him: 'Champion of Champions.'

But there is only one question I now need to find the answer to. Will any of these powerful memories be enough to save my career tomorrow? And the truth is, I honestly don't know. What I do know, though, is that I need to finish in the top ten of finishers to have any chance of saving my career, which on current form appears unlikely to say the least. I have had a top ten finish once ... but that was three years ago, before the terrible crash just a week later, when I was hit by a TV car who didn't see me, throwing me onto a barbed wire fence and down a steep ravine. I broke my leg, wrist and collarbone in that one, to add to a host of other injuries I'd had up to that point in my career.

But, if nothing else, I have something that can be quite powerful in the sporting world, hope. Why? I can almost hear you ask. Why should tomorrow be any different from the last three years that have contained so many bitter disappointments and ultimate failures? Well, it's quite simple really, the reason I have hope is because the race takes place in Italy, a country that I have never raced in professionally before. I may never have raced here, but I have trained here many times and there's just something special about this fantastic country, something about its roads, its hills and mountains that brings out the very best in me. I feel at home here. It was actually in this land of legends that I first began to learn, and first began to dream with an old man who inspired me with memories of a Champion of long ago.

So, it's simple. For me to have success tomorrow, it's vital that I remember those lessons from the old man and remember those wonderful, youthful dreams that occurred during three eventful weeks of my teenage life. I have to dredge up those three weeks that happened the summer following my humiliating capitulation at the school sports day on that sorry afternoon that haunts me still. I need to recall the lessons of those three weeks that were to change my life and helped transform me from a teenager who thought he knew it all, to one who at the very least was prepared to listen and learn and make the best of himself. If I can somehow manage to summon up all those happy, painful, inspirational, tragic yet ultimately uplifting memories of that crucial period in my life and drag them forward to the very front of my mind, then maybe, just maybe, I'll have a chance of pulling off a shock and saving the career I love and the one that I know I was born to do.

I simply must remember those three weeks...

1

*

IT was summer 2002, but there had been plenty of water under the bridge prior to me embarking on a three week holiday with my father, who, up until then, had been a very distant figure in my life. I didn't really know him, in fact, I didn't really like him. You see, my mother and father had split up when I was about four years old. I don't remember much about it, I don't actually remember much about him being there at all, in fact, my main memories of my father up to that eventful summer of '02 are based upon being picked up by him every other Saturday morning from my mum's house in Three Crosses – usually at the stupidly early time of half past eight – and then being driven to his Cardiff flat in silence, after the usual boring conversation ... 'How's school?', 'How's your mother?', 'Are you giving her enough help?', 'Are you doing your homework?' ... had quickly ended.

Our journeys swiftly became defined by this awkward hush and lack of conversation, interrupted only by the sounds coming from Dad's Toyota's flash CD player, belting out the latest CD from The Stereophonics – *Just Enough Education to Perform* – my favourite band.

The reason I disliked my own father was nothing to do with the split between him and my mother. In fact, as far as I could tell at the time, they still pretty much liked each other. They always greeted themselves with a hug and a kiss, and to be honest, I seemed to get in the way as I'd stand there in the hallway waiting to leave, blue adidas kit bag slung over my shoulder. As I waited, I would gaze lovingly at my bike which I knew I wouldn't be able to ride until at least the following afternoon, when I would return from Cardiff, the city I hated going to because I had to go there with my father. My father who lived in a posh flat in Cardiff Bay where everything was in place and where I had to be tidy. My father who could never find anything to say to me unless it involved a question about whether I was doing something properly or behaving myself. My father who wouldn't let me do as I wanted like my mum did. My father who hated sport, but especially my own sporting love, cycling.

Looking back, his total hatred of sport was the main reason for my dislike of him. I absolutely and totally loved sport and everything about it. I really liked music and watching TV too, but sport was really what I cared about most, sometimes to the exclusion of everything else. On TV, I watched anything and everything I could that featured a sport – football, rugby union, golf, tennis, cricket, Formula One ...everything. Well, apart from horse racing that is, I really couldn't stand that, it was so totally pointless and boring. I did quite enjoy the Grand National, but that was always down to my mum who watched it every year and always managed to find a horse's name similar to someone she knew, which she would then bet on in the race. She'd spend the fifteen minutes it took for the race to start and finish by jumping up and down screaming at the horse she had picked, not ever really knowing which one it was! But for all her screaming and shouting, the only time I remember her winning was when I was about seven and she picked a horse that was named after her Auntie Minnie – Minnehoma it was called. That day was also memorable as it was also the last time I remember her and my dad having an argument. He'd been gone for a few years by then, but Mum had asked him to spend the day with us, as he often still did up to that point, so that we could all watch the race together as a family. I liked that back then. However, before the race, Dad got really angry for some reason when the TV people did a feature about a famous jockey called Peter Scudamore who had a twelve year old son called Tom who was apparently very talented and being trained by his dad to become a jockey too. Even the grandfather of the family, Michael Scudamore, had been a famous jockey. I thought it was really cool and liked the idea of being the son of a famous sportsman who could then follow in his dad's – and granddad's – footsteps and make everyone proud. As the feature was being shown and they were interviewing the three of them, I just remember my dad getting angrier and angrier making increasingly stroppy comments resulting in my mum having a real go at him about 'Letting it go' and 'moving on for God's sake' – whatever that all meant. It soon ended in Dad walking out without seeing Mum finally win her bet as Minnehoma romped home. I didn't care though. Mum bought us tea from the chippie in Sketty Park with her winnings – two battered sausages, small pie and chips, with dandelion and burdock – result! But Grand National apart, horse racing was not for me.

But cycling? Well, that was another story. I absolutely loved it. My big hero was 'Big Mig' – Miguel Indurain, a huge Spaniard who had won the Tour de France five times in a row up to 1995. My best mate Jamie and I had started watching the cycling after seeing Chris Boardman on TV riding his 'Superman' bike. The two of us had been outside in the garden playing football when Jamie's dad called us in 'to see the fastest cyclist in the world'. From that day, our interest in cycling began, and before long, Jamie and I became totally hooked. When cycling's biggest race, the Tour de France was televised in July, we'd rush home every day from our school in Three Crosses, just in time to watch the last hour or so of that day's stage. Throughout our childhood, the Tour de France became the centre of our fascination, especially listening to the commentary by Phil Liggett and Paul Sherwen, and it seemed in those early days that 'Big Mig' won nearly every single day. I worshipped him totally. Some people in school idolised Neil Jenkins, Ryan Giggs or Lennox Lewis, but Jamie and me idolised this huge Spanish cyclist that nobody else in school had ever even heard of. As a result of this, the rest of our mates thought we were both nuts. Even though we were both in the school football and cricket teams, cycling remained our major interest. When all the other lads had a kick about after school or on weekends, Jamie and I would join them initially, only to get a bit bored after about twenty minutes, when the lure of our bikes became too great. We'd make our excuses, before jumping aboard and heading for the quiet country lanes of Cilonen, where we'd pretend we were racing through the French countryside at the head of the peloton – the pack – taking it in turns to be 'Big Mig' or our other favourite, the stylish French climber, Richard Virenque. If ever I was stopped from cycling in those days because of the weather or when it was dark during the wintertime, my disappointment knew no bounds. I was gutted. I loved it that much.

And that love of cycling I had developed so completely was the real reason why I didn't get on with my dad. Because he didn't love it at all, in fact, he absolutely hated cycling.

He never bothered to explain to me why he disliked it so much, he simply never even spoke about it. The hardest issue I had to deal with back then in terms of our relationship, was that he took no interest in my love of sport whatsoever. We rarely had a kickabout in the park like a normal father and son, he'd never make a point of watching a big football match on TV like the FA Cup Final or even a Wales Rugby International, and as regards cycling, well, whenever I mentioned it or made reference to it, he changed the subject immediately. It was always out of bounds as a topic of conversation as far as he was concerned. So, every other weekend, when I was forced to stay with him in Cardiff, the sad reality for me was that my bike remained parked in the hallway back in Swansea, idle. And it wasn't just the physical side of cycling that was denied me when I was with him either, there were never any conversations of 'Big Mig', Richard Virenque or 'Superman' Chris Boardman to entertain me either. In time, I'd learned to accept the harsh fact that, as far as my father was concerned, cycling was off the agenda. He hated it, and he hated it so much that I'd began to believe that he hated me for loving it. It wasn't a nice time.

2

*

SO that was me and my dad. Not great. Looking back, I guess part of me really wanted us to get on well, but the very fact that we didn't, never really bothered me that much to be honest. I was less interested in worrying about the relationship I had with my father, than I was about having fun, and that mostly involved my best mate Jamie and it usually concerned cycling.

One day in particular ended with the biggest row I ever had in my life off my mother and, predictably, it was all Jamie's fault. We were about ten years old and bored. It was the summer holidays of 1999 and the rest of the boys were playing 'Test Match' cricket on the village green, known locally as The Banc. The previous day had been the longest stage in that year's Tour De France, 147 miles, ending in Albi in southern France. It wasn't just the longest stage, but it was lumpy (hilly) too. It was painful just watching it on TV! In tribute to this longest stage, Jamie decided that we should mark the occasion by riding our own mega-stage to copy the peloton, and his plan was to take off and go on the longest bike ride we'd ever been on. So, being meticulous planners, we went to the village shop for our energy supplies, bought a couple of bottles of pop, four bars of chocolate and two bananas before setting off down the Cilonen lanes. These lanes were our gateway to the glorious Gower Peninsula without having to negotiate the busy common roads. Usually, we'd just cycle through them until we came to a main road either where remote Welshmoor dropped down to the main North Gower road on the way to Llangennith, or alternatively the opposite way, where the lanes ended at the junction with Fairwood Common, behind the airport. These junctions marked the boundaries where we'd normally turn back and head for home. Not this day.

'Let's go to my Auntie's,' Jamie announced with a sneaky smile.

'Ok,' I said. 'Where's that?'

When he answered 'Port Eynon', its significance didn't really register. I'd been to Port Eynon of course, everyone who lived in Swansea had been there ... but because it's almost Gower's furthest point west, it was usually reached by car! I had no idea how far it actually was to Port Eynon from Three Crosses, but not worrying about mere details such as that, we'd calculated that the two Mars bars and banana each that we'd both bought would be plenty to get us there in terms of fuel.

So, at about 10.30am, without a care in the world and an adventure to be had ahead of us, off we went, cycling into the sun.

My first mistake? Not telling my mother of our plan. My second mistake? Not realising that Port Eynon was actually fifteen miles away. My third mistake? Not wearing padded shorts.

The first hour was fantastic.

We drifted through the lanes in an imaginary world of professional cyclists, taking it in turns to lead, slowing down to feed and drink, before speeding up again pretending to make lethal sprints that would separate us from our imaginary peloton. Once the sun was at its highest in the sky and I could feel its full effects, burning my pale face, I began to sense that we might just have bitten off more than we could chew. At the point of this worrying realisation, we were halfway up Cefn Bryn – a steep hill which is one of Gower's highest points – and I could hardly keep my legs going as Jamie surged ahead, so steep was the road becoming. It was one of those horrible moments when I really wanted to cry rather than carry on, and my pain was made worse by the increasing steepness of the hill, the cars that were flying dangerously past us, and also the fact that Jamie was tearing along and leaving me behind. I panicked and thought he was abandoning me, which brought an awful realisation right to the front of my mind – I had no real idea where his auntie lived! Feeling exposed and on the verge of tears, complete with quivering lip and a face scorching red from the power of the sun, a rage surged through me that I'd never felt before in my life. Suddenly, my legs started to move quicker and faster, and the anger generated a force and strength that I had never displayed on a bike before. It was a fantastic feeling but also the strangest sensation. Just moments earlier, my legs were so tired and aching to the point of me giving up and quitting, something I was quite used to doing, as you know. My feelings of desperation due to the fear of being abandoned were made worse by the pain I was feeling, especially in my calves, which were so tight that I thought I'd never catch Jamie. But once the anger had surged through me, I started to absolutely fly, suddenly free of pain and totally at one with my bike.

I'd never felt this way before, so free and in tune with my machine. So, I just kept my head down and went for it, getting closer to Jamie with every turn of the pedals, my feet pounding down on them until they seemed to be whirling in a blur. It seemed no time at all until I caught – and quickly flew past – Jamie, just as we got to the top of Cefn Bryn. Or so I thought.

As I gave my final effort to reach the peak of the hill ahead of Jamie, so I became aware of my desperate miscalculation. All I'd succeeded in reaching was a kink in the road that swung to the right which couldn't be seen from lower down the hill. As I realised this and looked up, I saw one final, long, steeper climb which had to be negotiated before I could say I had conquered my own, personal, mountain stage. The disappointment of that realisation hit me instantly, and the life just drained out of my legs quicker than it had surged into them just moments before. It was as if somebody had instantly turned off the energy tap within me. I couldn't even make one more turn of the pedals. I'd gone from Big Mig to Squealing Pig in a heartbeat. So once again, I quit. It was all I could manage to just put my feet down on the ground before both me and my bike toppled and fell over onto the side of the road together. Jamie caught me up and stopped.

'Steep isn't it, Danster?' he laughed. 'You didn't know about the final bit did you?'

'Shut up,' I panted and sat on the verge, crushed. 'How bloody far is Port Eynon anyway?'

'Not far,' lied Jamie, 'Let's have a rest for a couple of minutes and then we'll push the bikes up the rest of the hill.'

So we stayed off the road, sat on a grass bank and opened our bottles of pop, and guzzled the contents greedily. I've never forgotten the taste that day. Sweet, refreshing and as thirst quenching as anything I'd ever drunk in my life. With it gone, and on the back of possibly the biggest burp ever heard on Cefn Bryn, I realised that I needed some energy in the form of my one remaining chocolate bar. Or should I say milk shake. The heat of the sun combined with the warmth in my pocket had melted it almost totally. Still, energy boosts were important – I even understood that back then – so I opened the wrapper and did my best to suck out its gooey contents, pausing only briefly to prevent, in vain, half of it slide out of the wrapper and all down my brand new Nike blue T-shirt. Jamie laughed at this so much that some of his own chocolate went down the wrong way, the pop-chocolate mixture pouring from his nostrils as he tried to prevent himself choking to death. Despite the laughter that ensued, we both realised that we were not in particularly good shape.

But, even though we were feeling increasingly sorry for ourselves, one thing we weren't – we told ourselves – were quitters. Well, I was to be honest, but Jamie wasn't, so, unfortunately, that left me with no choice, so I went along with him, pretending to be keen. Fed and watered, off we went, walking slowly as we awkwardly pushed our bikes over the top of Cefn Bryn in silence, brought on by a combination of stomach ache, sunstroke, general fatigue and a feeling of being a very long way from home. Once over the top we got back on our bikes and glided down the other side, freewheeling into the village of Reynoldston. From there, it was a right turn through more leafy lanes until we passed the 'Port Eynon – 4 miles' sign. Four miles? I simply looked at the sign and realised something instantly and with total certainty – I just wanted to go home. But following Jamie's lead, I continued, and after what seemed an age, finally passed through the village of Scurlage before we eventually freewheeled downhill into Port Eynon. As wonderful as that moment felt, the cool breeze streaming into my face as I followed Jamie speeding down the hill – the very steep hill – into Port Eynon village, I began to feel even more uneasy. There's only one thought that goes through your mind as you shoot down a very steep hill ...'Oh God, I'm going to have to cycle back up this later on the way back'.

I tried to blank that extremely painful prospect out of my mind.

Finally, thankfully, Jamie slowed down and coasted right, into the driveway of his auntie's house overlooking the fantastic beach of Port Eynon.

'What's the time Jame?' I sighed, as I pulled my bike to a halt on the edge of his auntie's lawn. 'I think my mum wanted me home for lunch'.

'Bit late for that Danster,' he laughed. 'It's half past three.'

'Oh God,' I groaned. 'She's gonna kill me,' and I cursed quietly to myself as the realisation that it would take hours and hours to get back home kicked in. Added to this feeling of total desolation was the fact that I felt absolutely knackered, I had blisters on my hands and as for my backside, well, the less said about the state that was in, the better.

Pleasingly, Jamie's backside must have been in a similar state of disrepair to mine, because as he made his way up to his auntie's front door to ring the bell, he walked, bandy legged, like a baboon on one of David Attenborough's *Life on Earth* programmes.

He stopped at the door and rang the bell. No answer.

He waited, then rang again. No answer.

Even Jamie stopped smiling at this point, and nervously looked back over his shoulder at me to share his anxiety. He rang a third and final time.

No answer. His auntie wasn't even bloody in.

In complete despair, I flopped down on his auntie's lawn, where I was quickly joined by an equally glum Jamie who seemed to me to be on the verge of tears. Oddly, that made me feel a lot better.

'What are we gonna do?' I asked, quietly. 'I don't think I'll be able to sit back down on that saddle'.

The pained nod of agreement from Jamie the baboon boy, along with the unimpressed look on his face as he considered that particular pleasure, suggested he too was not ready to enjoy that treat for a little while longer yet.

So there we lolled, in total silence for about an hour, on Jamie's auntie's perfectly kept front lawn, under a baking sun, hardly speaking and just wondering or more accurately, worrying, about what we should do next.

Then, just as I was coming to terms with the fact that the only way out of this mess was going to be to jump on the bike, ride up that massive hill and begin our journey home, I heard the best sound I'd heard in a very, very long time. It was the sound of the horn of Jamie's auntie's VW Polo.

She pulled into the driveway, got out of the car smiling and waving, just managing to hide the shock of finding her beloved ten-year-old nephew and his chocolate covered, red faced mate on her lawn in various levels of distress. Looking at us with pity, she didn't question us, and instead just asked,

'Hiya boys, do you fancy some squash then?'

Our weary nods were reply enough.

Over a gallon of squash, some ham rolls and six Welsh cakes, we perked up no end. Then came the question that instantly left me cold.

'I'm surprised your mothers allowed you both to come this far, what did they say when you told them you were coming here then?'

Our sheepish lack of response told Jamie's auntie everything she needed to know.

'Oh my goodness boys ... they'll be worried sick. You'd better give them a ring straight away ... but I warn you, they'll be furious.' She walked into the lounge to show us the phone. Calling back to me she said: 'Daniel, you'd better come and ring yours first, I'll speak to Jamie's mum.'

'Where've you been?' my mother screamed down the line.

I told her.

'Port Eynon? Port Bloody Eynon?'

It was the first time I'd ever heard her swear.

'You are bloody grounded for a week.'

It was the first time I'd heard her say that too.

3

✳

I DIDN'T know it at the time, but the year after my abject humiliation in the school sports day 400m race, the summer of 2002 was starting to deliver the big changes that were would eventually alter my life forever.

About six months before that year's Tour de France began in Luxembourg, with the then unmasked cheat Armstrong winning the 4.3 mile time trial, my mum had met somebody who would, in time, become her boyfriend. I began hearing lots of whispered conversations from my mum's friends during that period in which she'd begun to see this man on a regular basis. Just before I'd walk into a room where Mum was having a cuppa with one of her mates or other, I'd overhear questions like 'What's Daniel going to make of him Alison, you know he can be a bit headstrong at times?' or, 'Do you think Daniel is going to accept him?' or, 'Do you think Rob is going to get on with Daniel, is he really going to understand how close you and Daniel are?'

I never gave it that much thought to be honest, it wasn't anything to do with me as far as I could see, it was up to my mum what she did, so I just didn't bother much about it all. In the early days when I saw Rob parking his car, I would often go straight out to play to avoid him. Maybe I was hoping that he would just go away, but before long I just got used to having this bloke pop round to see my mum from time to time. And, as far as I was concerned, that was as far as it went.

But that was in the early days. By July of 2002, he'd been on the scene for about six months, and the more I got used to Rob being around, the more I began to grow to like him. Then, one evening, as I sat eating the burger and chips meal I'd nagged Mum to get for me,

I could tell from the way that she'd gone all quiet that she had something on her mind. I sensed something was up – it was obviously time for a talk. Mum started it.

'Dan, you know I've been seeing quite a lot of Rob, don't you?'

'Yes,' I replied, pretending not to be interested.

'Well, we're all going to be seeing him more often from now on. Is that okay love?'

'Suppose so,' I said as I kept concentrating on the burger I was demolishing without looking up.

What I really wanted to do was put the burger down, look her straight in the eye and ask plainly what was going on? Was Rob going to move in? Was Rob going to marry her? Was Rob going to become my dad? But instead, I just carried on eating my burger and continued avoiding her eyes at all costs. Looking back, I don't know why I was being evasive, I actually really liked Rob. In fact, there was nothing not to like. He was funny, he was kind and he loved sport and in particular, football. Apparently he used to play for Swansea City's youth team and once played for their reserves when he was 17 and had shown me the programme – it was against Queens Park Rangers ... I was dead impressed. Les Ferdinand had even played against him. Rob didn't play anymore, because, well, he was really fat, but he would often call round the house when there was a live game on TV, bring a couple of cans of coke and a tin of hot dogs. I never really worked out why, but he always kept going on about football all being about 'the smell of the hotdogs' whatever he meant by that. Still, we'd sit together, watch the game and eat the hot dogs. I loved them. My record was eight.

So, when Mum was going through her speech about how Rob was going to become a bigger part of the family, I didn't really worry about it too much. I was just glad she was happy. Then she said: 'How do you think your dad will take it?'

I was a little surprised by the question, looked up and saw that she was upset. I said nothing and looked quickly away.

After a pause, she continued: 'I'm really sorry it didn't work out between your dad and me Dan ... I really am.' She looked down at me and a single tear fell onto her cheek.

'We both really loved each other when we had you, and we both loved you too. You should always remember that.'

I was getting quite embarrassed now and starting to squirm a little. I didn't want to hear stuff like this – what was she thinking of? I did understand what she was saying and when she went on about them really loving me, well, frankly it had never occurred to me that they hadn't. I mean, shock news, my mum and dad loved me – well, that was their job wasn't it? In between the embarrassing pauses and my squirming, I did however give what she was saying some thought. I loved my mum, and I guess I loved my dad too – in a way – but now as my mum had brought the subject up, if I was being honest about it, I probably liked Rob quite a bit more than I did my dad. I knew that was not very fair on my dad, but that's just how I felt at the time. Rob was fun and played football with me and turned up once a week with a tin of hotdogs – Dad didn't. In fact, I don't think I'd ever even seen him near a hotdog.

'Oh I'm sorry love, I knew I'd get upset,' Mum said, dabbing away the tears. 'I just want you to know that your dad and me will always love you and Rob will too.'

Another pause.

'Are you sure you're going to be all right about all of this?'

'Yes,' I mumbled, embarrassed, as I shoved the last chunk of burger in my mouth. 'Can I go out now? Jamie and me are going down Cilonen on the bikes.'

My mother smiled, 'Yes of course ... so long as it's only Cilonen mind ... I still haven't forgiven you for your Port Eynon jaunt!' and she came over and kissed me as I made my way out of the back door to grab my bike. I couldn't wait to get out of there.

Within minutes I'd forgotten about the conversation and was flying up Pant-y-Dwr to call for Jamie, blissfully unaware that the awkward conversation I had just had with my mum was about to set in place a chain of events that would change, not just my life, but the lives of those closest to me forever. But as I flew up the road to Jamie's I had no understanding of that. Instead, as ever, I was turning the pedals in the style of Big Mig and my other new hero, Germany's young Olympic road race champion, Jan Ullrich, and imagining that I was one of them, sprinting to yet another stage victory in the imaginary Tour de France of my mind.

4

✳

A WEEK or so later, following another day with Jamie out on the bikes, finishing with tea at his house, I left him and made my short way home. As I freewheeled around the corner into Coed Lan, I saw Rob's Mercedes parked outside our council house – always a funny picture I thought, seeing it wedged in between the rusty Ford Fiestas and hub-cap-less Fiat Pandas – and pedalled a bit quicker to see him. The thought of the hot dogs were always a big motivation to me.

I threw down my bike on the front grass and ran in, slightly startling Rob and Mum, who swung round in surprise. I saw instantly that there were no hotdogs, just a bottle of champagne and two glasses. 'Something's up here,' I thought.

'Hello mate,' laughed Rob, as he walked toward me and ruffled my hair, before giving me a hug. 'Your mum's got a bit of news for you.'

Mum looked a bit serious as she sat down on the settee and called me over to sit next to her.

'Look love, I hope you don't mind what I'm about to tell you, but before you make an opinion, you've got to understand that it's been quite hard for me this last couple of years and ... um ... whilst I've never moaned about it, I've never really had much time to myself and ... erm ... you know that everything I've ever had, I've given to you. You know that don't you Dan?' She was rambling by this point, so paused, glanced at Rob who nodded to her with assurance, then continued. 'Well, I just wanted to tell you that Rob's asked me to go on holiday with him ... abroad. On holiday ... abroad.'

I got the picture. Abroad.

God, is that all? I'd thought I was going to be faced with the full-on marriage speech.

'We're going to the Caribbean for three weeks,' said Rob. 'Isn't that fantastic for your mum?'

Three weeks? I thought.

'Three weeks?' I said. 'What am I going to do for three weeks?' I asked, now not quite so relaxed about the prospect.

As my mum struggled for an answer, I thought about what they were saying to me and far more importantly, what the implications were, realising that I didn't really mind, mainly because I knew what was coming. I was certain that she was about to tell me that she'd rung Jamie's mum Julie, her best friend, and that she was about to announce that I'd be staying with them for three weeks. That suited me down to the ground. I loved Jamie, he was my best mate, his mum and dad were a great laugh, and, even though this was still my little secret that I hadn't mentioned to anyone, I totally fancied his gorgeous sister, Catherine. So, all good. In fact, all very good! You two have a great time and see you in three weeks, I thought.

To be honest, the more thought I gave it, the more I figured that I'd rather stay with Jamie and his family – not to mention our bikes and the unlimited cycling opportunities we'd have – for three weeks than go to the Caribbean with Mum and Rob anyway. I knew I'd just feel like a spare part, getting in the way of the two lovebirds if I went with them.

Then, out of the blue came the final, completely game changing, comment.

'While we are away, you'll be going to stay in Cardiff with your father.'

Her words hit me like a jackhammer. I went cold.

'I've just come off the phone to him,' she said. 'He's finishing a big contract this week and then he doesn't have to work until September when his next contract starts, so he's going to have you while we're away. That'll be really nice for you both won't it?'

I remained cold. I didn't say a word.

'Hey mate, it'll be fine,' chirped Rob, sensing my deep disappointment. 'You can take your bike with you, there's some nice parks in Cardiff. There's a really nice track up along the river behind the castle towards the cricket ground.'

I interrupted rudely. 'My dad doesn't have a bike and doesn't let me take mine there in case it dirties the flat. So there'll be no cycling will there?' I was angry.

Rob looked away, blushing, embarrassed and began focussing his stare on the bubbles still bursting in his champagne glass.

Close to tears and fuming, I got up from the settee, glanced at Mum with disgust, then looked down to the floor, walked out and straight up the stairs to my bedroom without saying a word.

I lay back on my bed and fought back the tears. Three weeks. Three weeks without my bike and worse, three weeks with my dad. The dad I didn't get on with. The dad that didn't like sport. The dad that didn't let me ride my bike. The dad I hated.

I looked up at the huge poster I had of Big Mig pinned to my ceiling, the one of him out of the saddle, massive tanned legs pumping in his Banesto shorts topped off by the leaders yellow jersey. In it, his bronzed face was a serious look of concentration, covered in sweat with his coal black eyes just staring up at the hill ahead as the rest of his opponents wilted down it, out of focus, dropping further and further behind. Broken.

I knew how they all felt.

I also looked at the smaller picture I'd wedged in the dressing table mirror of my other hero Ullrich, standing on the podium in Paris in his winners yellow jersey of 1997, one of the youngest Kings of the Tour de France in history. My cycling inspiration, along with Big Mig.

As I looked back and forth between both pictures, through increasingly tear-blurred eyes, I wondered if they'd ever had to abandon their bikes for three weeks to go and stay with a stupid father they didn't even like.

Never, I thought.

5

✳

NEXT morning, as I sat in my bedroom reading my official 2002 Tour de France magazine – outlining all the details of the teams, stages and climbs – I heard the phone ringing downstairs.

I was coming to terms with Mum's bombshell of the previous day outlining my stay with Dad, and as gutted as I still was, I was finally beginning to accept it. Part of this was because I knew I had no option. The more I thought about it, the more I tried to tell myself that it wasn't going to be as bad I thought – he was my dad after all, so I figured I could cope. However, if I'm being totally honest, the real reason behind my grudging acceptance was that already that morning I had been able to pop out and see Jamie, talk the whole sorry mess through with him, and together, we had hatched a plan. We'd found out that the reason I was having to stay with my dad and not Jamie and his family, was that they were all going on holiday for a week to Benalmadena in Spain, the day before Mum was due to fly off to the Caribbean. But, Jamie had worked out that because they were only going for ten days, they'd all be back by the middle of my second week with Dad, which meant there was no reason whatsoever why I couldn't then return from Cardiff and stay with Jamie for the last week and a half of Mum's break. All I had to do now, was wait for the right moment to lay it on thick to Mum that I really didn't want to be away from all my friends – and my bike – for three weeks of the summer holidays, so could I please come back and stay with Jamie after about ten days in Cardiff with Dad? That way, I'd be spending some time with my dad, but would then get to enjoy myself for at least half the time Mum was in the Caribbean enjoying herself with Rob. That was a pretty reasonable deal in my opinion. I also knew that Mum was usually happy for me to get my own way in most situations, so all I had to do was convince her that Dad didn't really want me with him for three weeks anyway, and because I'd stayed with Jamie loads of times before, there wasn't a problem with me staying with him again, and I'd get to spend some time with Catherine too! Outstanding. I was quite impressed with myself.

Then Mum shouted up from downstairs,

'Dan, it's your father ... he's got some news for you.'

Great, I thought, now might be the perfect time to put my strategy into action. Once I'd laid my plans out for Dad, who was bound to agree, it would just be a question of Mum speaking to Julie to arrange my stay. Simple. I was still feeling quite pleased with myself as I skipped down the stairs and took the phone off Mum, and was much chirpier than I normally was when I spoke to my father on the phone.

'Hi, Dad.' I almost sung into the phone

'Hello son – how are you?'

'Fine thanks Dad, how are you?'

'Very good son, nice to hear you sounding so happy ... for a change. Has your mother told you the news?'

'Yeah. I was going to talk to you about that Dad.' I was waiting for the right moment, but what the hell, this seemed to be it.

'Oh yes, what did you want to say?' Dad replied, with some concern in his voice.

'Well, you know Jamie is going to be back home from his holidays when I'm with you?'

'Mmmm, yes' pondered my father.

'Well, I was wondering if you couldn't bring me back down here after about ten days so that I can stay with him for the rest of the time that Mum's away, so we can go and see our mates and stuff. You know, it is summer holidays after all, and three weeks out of that when we only get six is quite a lot. Will that be ok?'

Another 'Mmmm,' followed, which I didn't take as a sign of good news. 'Well normally, it wouldn't be too much of a problem son, but I'm a little confused. I thought you said you're mother had told you the news?'

'She has,' I replied, equally confused. 'I'm coming up to Cardiff with you for three weeks next Tuesday while she's away with Rob.'

'Typical,' said my dad sternly, 'she hasn't told you.'

I sensed my cunning plan was beginning to unravel.

'Told me what?' I asked, coldly and impatiently

'That I'm taking you to Italy.'

I was stunned into silence. For a moment anyway.

'Italy! Italy?' I shouted. 'Why?'

'Well you've never been for a start have you?' he snapped. 'Besides,' he said more calmly, 'I've got to go back to deal with some family business – I haven't been for so long and there's some problems I've got to sort out. That's why I've taken time off work until September. I told your mother that I could look after you, but that it would have to be in Italy. I'm sorry if that doesn't fit in with your plans, but I'm not the one gallivanting to the Caribbean for three weeks.'

Ignoring his obvious pop at my mother, I was gutted. I didn't even want to go to Cardiff, let alone Italy. At least there was a small chance he might let me take my bike to Cardiff if I nagged him enough, but not to Italy. No chance. I bet they hardly even cycled there – apart from Marco Pantani who won the last Tour de France before the cheating Armstrong's dominance began, who'd ever heard of an Italian cyclist? Everyone knew the best were French or Spanish, Pantani had just got lucky. All of a sudden I felt really angry and frustrated. So I exploded.

'Well, she never told me and I'm not going! I don't want to go to Italy, I didn't even want to go to Cardiff ... in fact, I don't want to go anywhere with you!'

I just dropped the phone on the floor and ran upstairs. From the landing, I heard my mother apologising to my father and promising to start to try to sort the situation out. I just shut my bedroom door and buried my head in my pillow crying with frustration. I had never been so disappointed ... or angry, ever before. I began shaking with rage.

6

*

BEFORE I go on, there's one small question that you are probably asking yourself, and it needs a little explaining.

Why Italy?

Okay, let me shed some light on my family background, it's a little unusual. As you already know, my name is Daniel. In common with many people with that name, most people call me Dan or Danny – apart from Jamie of course, who insisted on calling me 'the Danster' – but I'm a Dan or Danny to pretty much everyone else. But not on my birth certificate. That reads Danilo.

Danilo Roberto Rossi.

Italian. Well fifty per cent Italian anyway

You see, my father's name is Gianluca Rossi, known to everyone, except me, as Luca. He's one hundred per cent Italian.

My dad came to Swansea University when he was nineteen and met my mother, who was then Alison Williams. Eventually, they fell in love, got married, had me, fell out of love and divorced. All by the time I was four years old. My mum then dropped the Rossi, reverted back to her maiden name and we moved from one side of Swansea – Brynhyfryd – to the other, Three Crosses. Two days later, Danilo Roberto Rossi, was introduced to his new school friends in the small Gower village school of Crwys Primary in Three Crosses as Daniel Robert Williams ... Danny Williams to nearly everyone. As time moved on, there were occasions when I forgot completely that I had such strong Italian roots, and that suited me fine. They held absolutely no relevance for me. I had no connections to Italy, had never met any of my dad's family and as far as I knew, my dad had never even been back to Italy since he arrived in Swansea all those years earlier. It was never even a talking point. Until I was about twelve, I had no idea why he had ended up in Swansea – I never thought to ask. Growing up, Mum always told me that when she and Dad were together, neither of them ever had much money, and because of that, summer holidays were always spent at home going to the wonderful Gower beaches ... it was no hardship to me, all that sea and sand! Still, despite the obvious attraction of going to Italy, it never became an option or an issue for them because it was never really affordable. In the last few years since the split, Dad had really started to do well for himself as an architect so I just sort of assumed that he'd been back to Italy at some point, now that he could afford it, but it never occurred to me to ask. The whole 'Italy' issue was simply not important to me. In addition, he'd never told me anything at all about the family back in Italy or his life there before he left, which in turn meant that I never had a reason to ask. So, with that as the background, every passing year meant that Danilo Rossi faded from my mind and Danny Williams grew ever bigger in his place.

However, now with Mum and Rob chucking the biggest of spanners into the works, Italy was now very much back on the horizon, and I wasn't happy at all to see it there. So, when my mother mentioned it again later that evening, I decided it was time to set out my stall for her, in as mature a way as I could possibly muster.

'I don't want to go to stupid, stinking, minging Italy with him,' I shouted at her.

'Oh come on now Dan,' she replied, 'most teenage kids would love to go to Italy for a holiday. It's a beautiful place and a fabulous opportunity for someone your age.'

'Rubbish. It's not, and none of my mates would want to go either. You don't know what you're talking about,' I shouted back rudely. 'In fact, I can't think of anyone who would want to go to such a stupid place.'

'Now come on Dan, don't be cheeky. I know this wasn't what you probably wanted, but it will do you good to spend some time in Italy with your father. I always wanted to go when your dad and me were together, but he never wanted to.'

'I always thought it was because you never had any money,' I shot back at her cruelly.

She sighed: 'Well that was part of it love, but one year, when you were about three, we had enough money for the flights, and I really wanted to go, but your dad refused to.' My mother paused in thought for a moment. 'He's a very good man your father, Dan, but very proud too. That's why sometimes he finds it hard to be relaxed with you because part of him knows that you have a bit of a strained relationship. He finds it hard to show his feelings, which means he struggles to come to terms with the relationship he has with you. He's had a lot of disappointments in his life.'

'Welcome to the club,' I said.

'Now that's enough Dan,' Mum replied in a sterner tone. 'This trip to Italy is exactly what you both need.'

I wasn't buying that!

'Well, it's not what I need,' I spat, 'so I don't care. I'm not bloody going and that's that!' Turning, I began to walk out of the room.

'Daniel Williams ... you stop right there!!' screamed my mother.

I stopped. I'd never heard her shout so loud. And she never, ever called me Daniel.

'Have you any idea how hard it's been for me? she yelled, on the verge of tears. 'Have you any idea how difficult it is to bring up a teenage boy, alone? How dare you speak to me like that? I've given everything for you this last ten years since your dad and me split, so don't you ever speak to me like that again. Ever. Do you understand?'

She was now shaking with rage. I'd never seen her like that before. I didn't know what to say.

'Do you understand?' she screamed at me even louder, in complete and utter rage.

She was still shaking and tears flowed onto her cheeks.

'Yes,' I muttered, a little scared, staring at the carpet.

'Good, I hope so', she said, regaining control in her voice.

'Now listen, I understand that you may not be too happy about this and, if you really don't want to go that much, then I'll pick up that phone right now and ring Rob and tell him I'm not going to the Caribbean with him. I really will. But, honestly Dan, do you really want that to happen?'

At least she'd stopped shaking. She'd have started again if I'd said what I was thinking – yes!

After coming that close to taking up her offer, but wisely, I think, choosing to remain silent, I grudgingly shook my head before looking at her and speaking. 'Ok, I'll go. But don't expect me to enjoy it because I won't. But I'll go. And don't expect it to be for three weeks,' I muttered as I left the room.

'What did you say?' my mother asked

'Nothing. I'll go, that's all.'

And with that I turned away, walked out and considered my fate.

Italy. With my dad. To live with a bunch of people for three weeks who I didn't even know. Unbelievable. How on earth did this manage to happen? Yet again, I was gutted, really gutted, but more than that I was now angry. Very angry and determined. Despite not wanting to show my mother, I had already made my mind up that there was no way I was going to enjoy my trip. I was certain about that.

And that meant my dad wasn't going to enjoy it either.

There was simply no way I was going to allow that to happen.

7

✻

AS the plane left the runway at Cardiff Airport and climbed steeply into the clouds over the Bristol Channel on its way to Turin a week later, not much had changed for me. I knew I'd been behaving badly, and I knew what I had been doing was wrong, but when I kissed my mother goodbye that morning, it was as if the worst part of my personality came right to the surface, and if I am being honest, it didn't have too far to come. I had hardly looked at my dad let alone spoken to him, that morning, as he drove us away, out of Three Crosses on the first leg of our journey to the airport. After a few minutes of the usual questions, he finally took the hint, left me alone and apart from The Stereophonics as usual, the rest of the journey passed in silence.

We'd been in the air for about an hour I think, which was enough time for me to make the most of the meal (average) and unlimited pop (outstanding), when I noticed that my dad hadn't even touched his food. He saw me looking at his full plate, and when I glanced up at him he was staring right at me. Finally, he spoke.

'Right, there's something you should know before we go any further,' he said, without a hint of a smile on his face.

I looked away.

'Danilo,' – he always called me that when he was angry – 'look at me,' he snapped.

I gave him a sly sideways glance.

'It is time for me to be honest with you and, as you are now growing into a man, it's about time you dealt with some truth.' The controlled anger in his voice made his Italian accent sound even stronger than it usually did.

I must admit, I was taken a little bit by surprise. He'd never spoken to me with such an assertive tone of voice before. In fact, usually, he would just let me get on with it when I was grumpy and leave me well alone. In recent times, that was nearly all of the time.

'My son, sometimes you can be a spoilt little kid, and frankly, that embarrasses me. Your mother is a good woman, but she spoils you and if you are not careful you are going to grow into a very difficult person and that is not good.'

I couldn't believe what I was hearing. How could this man have the cheek to speak to me like this! Just because he was my father didn't give him the right to talk to me like this!

'Being your father gives me the right to talk to you like this.'

God, could he read minds now too!

'You will live by my rules for the next three weeks and you can like it or you can lump it. If you choose to continue to treat me with no respect, then that is exactly what you will get from me. No respect. Respect is earned, not given. Frankly Danilo, your behaviour is not just poor, but above all stupid. That is almost the saddest part for me because one thing I know you are not is stupid. So, I now place the ball in your court. I want you to become a son I can respect, but that outcome is in your own hands. You must know I will always love you, that will never change – but as for the rest, well, that is up to you. I suggest you give it some thought.'

And that was that! Dad just turned away, pushed his food to one side, picked up his book, flicked to the page which held his book mark and began to read. Unlike my mother who chose to shake whenever she gave me a ticking off, which frankly wasn't that often, Dad was as cool as a cucumber. If I wasn't so angry, I would have been quite impressed, but I was absolutely boiling. In fact worse, I was tamping! If he seriously thought his little speech was going to work he was sadly mistaken. Any chance he had of me making his three weeks some sort of father and son bonding holiday had just gone up in smoke, there and then at 32,000 feet, in the time it took for him to deliver his pathetic little speech. The more I thought about what he said, the angrier I got. I made my decision right then. If my dad thought I was spoilt then that's exactly what he and his family were going to see. His spoilt little son from Wales. Once they'd had three weeks of me playing the brat, then my Italian family, Italy and most of all, my dad would hopefully be out of my life forever. And I couldn't wait. I was that angry, I really couldn't wait. I was certain of that.

As I sat there, I began to shake.

8

*

THE hire car was making its way from Turin to the hills around Cassano Spinola, a small town near the region's capital, Alessandria, a trip of about seventy miles. In the two hours that had passed since my dad's harsh words on the plane, we had not spoken, so I was even more determined that I was going to teach him a lesson. He wouldn't even let me put *Performance and Cocktails* by the Stereophonics on the car's CD. Instead I had to put up with Italian radio with rubbish old pop songs. Mind you, one of the tracks was perfect for our run through the Italian countryside ... 'Road to Hell' by someone called Chris Rea.

As we went further and the signs indicating the way to Cassano Spinola grew more frequent, Dad spotted a picnic area ahead, indicated, and pulled the grey Fiat Bravo off the main highway and slowed to a halt in the corner of the car park, before turning the engine off. I just stared out of the window in silence, trying to avoid whatever was coming. Finally, he broke the silence.

'Danilo, this is it. We are not far now from the home of my father and so, you now have to make a choice. You can either continue as you have been for the last few years as a spoilt little boy who hates it when he can't get his own way, or, you can realise that part of growing up is dealing with disappointments, and choosing to just smile and get on with it.'

'What, like you?' I interrupted. The words spat from my mouth almost without thinking, and the sarcasm in my voice gave my taunt greater impact.

'What do you mean – like me?' my father responded angrily.

'When was the last time you just smiled and got on with it? I asked him. 'Never, that's when. Why have you never, ever let me have any fun with you? Ever since I can remember, you've always been grumpy and you've never wanted to have a laugh. You know I love sport – football, rugby, cricket – everything, yet you never take any interest in it, you never let me watch it or never even talk to me about it. With you it always has to be the sensible things ... "do your homework, keep this tidy, look after your mother" ... and then, when I get grumpy with you for not having fun, you are the one who acts like the spoilt child, not me. Jamie's dad is not like that, he has plenty of fun with us. Why can't you be more like him?'

The car instantly filled with silence as we both just sat and stared out of our windows.

Down below the picnic spot was a thin, winding country road with a couple of cyclists heading toward a hill about a mile further away. I thought I'd push my luck, now that it appeared I had his full attention. 'And another thing.' I said. 'What is it exactly that you hate about me and my cycling?'

My father looked at me, seeming as though he was about to speak, then instead just turned away. Whatever words he wanted to say remained stuck on his lips.

I carried on regardless. 'You know only too well it's the one thing above all other things I love in life and have you ever once arranged for us to go out for a ride together? Have you ever allowed me to bring the bike to Cardiff? No, never. So what is it? Why do you dislike me so much that you'd be so spiteful to prevent me doing the one thing I love? I thought fathers were supposed to encourage their sons to enjoy the things they are good at. Just because you were probably rubbish at cycling when you were my age doesn't mean that you have to take that out on me.'

Again silence, until he finally spoke.

'Danilo,' he said softly. 'I don't dislike you and it hurts me so much that you think I do. You must understand, I am your father and I love you, but that doesn't mean that I have to approve of your behaviour. You may be right. I choose to give you discipline more than fun, and it is true I have no time for childish games and from this I will never change, so you will just have to get used to it. However, one day you may thank me I hope. If not, then I will have failed and that will be sad. So, I tell you again, you now have a choice – you can begin to grow up and make me proud in front of my family, or you can continue as you are and embarrass me. It is simple, the choice is up to you.'

'Yeah, it is up to me,' I fired back, still staring straight ahead, out of the window.

From the corner of my eye, I could see that my father looked at me for a moment before turning away, shaking his head slightly and letting out a long sigh. He then looked behind him, started the engine and reversed out of the parking space, the Fiat's wheels crunching over the stones in the car park. As he did so, music from the Italian radio station spat into life – 'Hotel California'. I decided it would be the perfect moment to leave my dad in no doubt what choice I was going to make. I pushed in my Stereophonics CD and turned it right up, 'The Bartender and the Thief' blaring straight out. My father just carried on driving. It was going to be a long three weeks, but now I just didn't give a monkey's and, even if I did, it was too late anyway.

I'd made my choice.

9

*

THE Fiat Bravo drove quietly around the main square of Cassano Spinola before my father found the narrow road he needed. It took him a further mile out of the town, to where the built-up houses and bungalows became less and less. Soon, we came to a junction in the road, where he continued right for half a mile further and then took a swinging left into a long driveway. At the end of this drive was a small courtyard, covered in gravel, in front of a fair-sized farmhouse with several outbuildings, a lovely stone water fountain at its centre. Like most of the surrounding buildings, the fountain was very old and in need of repair. Even in my bad mood I could appreciate that this was a beautiful setting, but if my father thought its loveliness would draw some positive sort of reaction from me, he was mistaken.

He turned off the engine, and the loud sound of Kelly Jones's raw vocals was instantly replaced by the quacking of ducks and geese who filled a small pond that stood to the left of the biggest of the four outbuildings. As soon as I got out, the ducks started to waddle and quack their way over, to find out who this stranger was.

'Nice aren't they? There used to be a much larger pond over there,' my father said, pointing to an area near the old shed, 'which usually had twice as many birds. Looks like it's been filled in recently. That's a shame isn't it?'

I ignored him. He walked over to me, seemingly ignoring the fact that we hadn't spoken for nearly an hour.

'Right, come on, let's go and meet the family. They're expecting us and are really excited to meet you.'

Again, nothing from me.

We walked toward the three raised steps that led to the huge oak door that was at the front of the farmhouse. Just as Dad was about to pick up the huge rusty iron knocker that sat right in the middle of the door, it swung open, and an old woman – around 70, white haired and dark skinned, dressed in an old fashioned black dress, with a lace edged apron – threw it opened and screamed.

'*Luca, Luca, mio figlio, mio figlio , si sono tornati!*'

She threw her arms around my father and shrieked and cried, hugging him so tightly he had to restrain her after about 30 seconds held in her vice-like grip.

'Mama, Mama,' he laughed, before speaking Italian to her that I assumed, judging by his actions, meant he was telling her that she had nearly killed him with her massive hug.

For the next three minutes, interspersed with hugs, tears and laughter, this old woman and my dad spoke non-stop in Italian. They spoke so fast, I have no idea how they could understand each other. I was almost certain that I saw my dad wipe away a tear at one point, but when he saw me looking, he turned quickly away.

Through it all, I tried to avoid showing any interest in what was unfolding in front of me, and just stood there, attempting to give the aloof impression that I saw these sorts of greetings every day of the week.

Then, Dad must have remembered that I was there. He grabbed the old woman's hand, and spoke in Italian, repeating straight after in English so that I could understand, a process he kept up throughout the reunions with his family that I had to endure over the ten minutes that followed.

'Mama, this is my son. Please meet your grandson, Danilo Rossi.'

'Daniel Williams,' I said coldly as the old lady embraced me and kissed me, while I stood still and cold as marble.

She didn't seem to notice my attempted dig at my dad – why would she I thought, she doesn't speak English. I realised I might find it a little harder than I'd thought to get across to the family the fact that I didn't want to be there and didn't want to be any part of them.

After I survived the near asphyxiation of my grandmother's chest crushing hug, I was introduced – in no particular order – to my great aunt and uncle, then my father's two sisters and their husbands, three cousins, who irritatingly were a lot younger than me, and a person called Elsa, who appeared to be some sort of maid or servant who my father seemed particularly fond of. Through it all, I noticed a scruffy old man who remained out on the back porch, seemingly distant to all the excitement generated by our arrival, and pretty much staying out of everyone's way.

Soon, the wine was opened and my father began drinking the large glass of red he'd been handed by one of his sisters. After a short while, I saw him motion toward the old man who was still outside, before saying something in Italian to his sister, who just shook her head and looked sadly back at my father. My father gave a big tut, seemed to curse, and turned to me.

'Danilo, I must go to speak with my father. Please wait here.'

Your father? I thought, being careful not to let my face betray my instant curiosity. Instead, I just shrugged.

I watched my dad as he walked toward the old fashioned stable type door, that led out onto the back porch, put down his glass of wine on the table as he passed, paused as he swung open the bottom half of the door and then took a deep breath as he took a stride out into the sunlight.

I could just about hear him say to the old man 'Papa' followed by something else that was short, but in Italian.

The two men barely looked at each other, then my father's father said something to my dad, again in Italian. Nothing more was spoken, and then after the briefest of glances, both men walked away from each other, my father back into the kitchen, and the old man alone down the garden path, toward a hedge that looked as though it stood on the banks of a small river.

The kitchen now stood in total silence.

Dad came back in and picked up his wine and took a swig. His mother walked toward him, said something that I assumed to be 'I'm sorry,' kissed him and gave him another hug. She then turned to me and spoke.

'She wants to know if you want some lemonade?' said my father.

'No,' I replied quickly, even though I was gasping. 'I just want to take my stuff to my room.'

My father translated to the room full of my relatives, and I could tell from the disapproving raised eyebrows of one or two of the adults that my plan was beginning to work.

Great, this spoilt brat will be out of here by the end of the week, I thought.

10

❊

I'D been shown to the bedroom at the back of the house that I was to use for the next three weeks. I didn't even bother unpacking my case ... there was no way I was going to be there that long. Annoyingly, I had to share the room with my father. But, as disappointed as I was not to have my own room, in a way I was pleased because I figured the more time I spent with my dad, the more I would annoy him, and therefore, the more chance there was of him getting totally fed up, giving in and getting me away from that place. The sooner the better.

I wandered over to the window and looked out at the view of the Italian countryside that laid itself out in front of me.

It was breathtaking.

The fields just stretched out for miles, a patchwork of differing shades filled with crops of every colour and description – one was just a blaze of yellow provided by the mass of sunflowers it contained – all separated by a network of winding country lanes. Instantly I thought of Cilonen, but it was so much better than that, this was a far grander version of those lanes in Three Crosses that Jamie and I had covered with such enjoyment almost every day for the many previous years. As I looked out, the lanes seemed endless. Some disappeared beneath high, thick green hedges only to re-appear a little further on as they emerged from the many dips and rises that the rolling landscape contained. In the far distance, about five or ten miles away I guessed, the scenery changed and hills seemed to sprout out of the flat ground and eventually soared to grow as big as mountains as the horizon made it hard to distinguish between the haze at the top of the uplands and the blue beginnings of the perfect clear sky.

And there, in the middle of it all, was a bunch of cyclists.

I tried to count them, but they were a little too far away for me to be certain, but I reckoned there were at least ten – maybe as many as twenty – cycling along one of the deserted roads, at pace, and swapping positions every two or three minutes, exactly as they did in the Tour de France peloton on TV. I was transfixed. The sheer excitement this scene threw into my mind almost took my breath away. I would have done anything – there and then – to be able to be dropped into the middle of them on a brand new Specialized racing bike to become part of that group, speeding along through the middle of this perfect cycling location. If only.

As I absorbed this magnificent sight and allowed my dreams to expand more and more, I noticed the scruffy old man down at the far end of the garden. The same scruffy old man that had taken part in that weird meeting with my father less than an hour before.

My grandfather.

I must admit I thought it was a bit odd that he hadn't said anything to me when we first arrived, but I guess he may not have known that I was there as he never even looked in through the kitchen window when all the greetings were taking place, as far as I could remember. Still, I wasn't that fussed. My plan was to get out of there as soon as I could, and for that to happen the less I had to do with everyone, the better. So instead of going down and seeing him, introducing myself to my own grandfather, I just stood there, watching him looking out at the glorious countryside that he must have known so well.

'His name is Umberto. He's your grandfather.'

I was so lost in my thoughts, that I jumped as high as the ceiling on hearing my father's voice.

Embarrassed and startled, I dropped my guard for a moment, and laughing, shouted at my dad: 'For God's sake, Dad – you nearly gave me a heart attack!'

'Nice to see you smiling at last. I'm sorry, I didn't mean to startle you.'

I was really annoyed at myself that I'd let my mask of misery slip so easily, and quickly lost the smile before turning away from my father, ordering him to knock when he came into the bedroom next time.

I heard him sigh behind me.

'Please go and see him,' he said nodding at my grandfather. 'The problem is between me and him, not you. I know he's really looking forward to meeting you.'

'He told you that did he?' I asked curtly.

'No, he didn't actually, Mama did. So please, forget about the issues you have with me, just go down and see him. Just say hello.'

I shrugged my shoulders, stood rooted to the spot for a few moments then turned, and walked towards the door. Then I stopped and turned round to look at my dad.

'What exactly is it between you two then? Why don't you get on?'

My father's face hardened slightly and when he spoke it was through thin, pursed lips.

'It's got nothing to do with you, so don't ever refer to it again.'

Yet another shrug for good measure and I was off, galloping down the first of the two flights of stairs until I saw my grandmother walking up the lower one, and slowed to a shuffle to continue with my impression that I didn't want to be there.

'Ah Danilo!' she shrieked as she put out her arms for yet another rib crushing hug, but this time I cruelly resisted, gave a very brief smile and walked past without acknowledging her any further. For the first time since I'd been there I felt quite guilty as I walked off and almost began to question my behaviour, but then I heard my father speaking to her in Italian and remembered my reasons, to get away from there – and him – as soon as possible.

I walked across the worn grey flagstones that provided the surface of the huge farmhouse kitchen, pushed open the stable door and emerged into the late afternoon sunshine. The lawn – or field as it more resembled – seemed much bigger to me than it had been when I had been looking down on it from the bedroom, and I could just about make out my grandfather, who had now moved, and was leaning against a huge cypress tree at the very bottom of the garden, that was providing him with shade from the heat of the sun.

Just as I started to walk down the lawn toward him, I was intercepted by one of my father's sisters, my aunt. I didn't know which one because I couldn't remember the names I'd been given earlier, but she knew me all right.

'Danilo!' she squealed in a loud Italian accent, '*come stai mio nipote?*'

I tried to ignore her and kept on moving.

'Danilo, please stop,' she said in English, a little more forcefully and with an extremely accented Italian voice. 'How you say? Umm, my brother seems very sad with you? Is this true Danilo?'

'Dunno ... don't care. And it's Daniel,' was my considered response, making certain I quickly picked out a blade of grass in the lawn by her feet, just focusing on it to make sure that I wasn't going to look up and into her questioning eyes.

'Danilo, please look at me.'

God, were they all mind readers in this family?

I ignored her plea and kept staring at the tiny, bent piece of grass that was the only thing in the world I was going to look at whilst this conversation took place.

'I can tell that your father is very sad and I do not think that you are being very nicely for him.'

I gave nothing, just stared at the blade of grass.

'What you are behaving like is not very nice and I cannot see why this way you would want to behave,' she continued in her broken Italian English way. 'Why, Danilo is it, why?'

Still nothing. I was trying to see if my gaze could penetrate the grass like the sun's rays through a magnifying glass when held over a piece of paper on a sunny day.

'You must know Danilo, we love your father ... my brother Luca, very, very much. He has not always had an easy life and I am sad that you do not like to help him in this way by being not nice. I hope that it is now time that you stop the bad ways and become nice for your father.'

Still nothing but my stare at the grass. I took the sound of her sigh as my cue to leave. As I looked up after turning to walk away down to the cypress tree and my grandfather, I noticed he was no longer there. Then, glancing to my right, I saw him – not more than twenty yards away – leaning against an old fence post, split in half and blackened as if it had been hit by lightning at some point in the past. My own, unknown grandfather, just looking straight at me. There was something about his eyes – even from that distance – the way that they peered straight at me, not in hatred or in love but somewhere in between. As if he knew.

I looked away, embarrassed, and pretended that I hadn't seen him, and carried on walking toward where I'd intended to go, down to the very bottom of the garden.

'Danilo – you stop now please,' called my aunt in her broken, Italian accented English, but as I continued to walk, I noticed from the corner of my eye my grandfather motion to her with swish of his hand to stop and my aunt immediately ceased speaking.

I walked a further ten or so paces, then briefly glanced over my shoulder, only to see my grandfather still looking at me, again, with those eyes. Those unsmiling eyes. He knew. And I also knew from that exact moment – he saw right through me.

My game was up. So I turned, and walked quietly back inside.

11

*

THE following morning I'd managed to avoid most people by pretending to be asleep when Dad got up for breakfast, and by the time I made it down stairs to the kitchen, a pitcher of milk along with some fresh bread and strawberry jam were left out on the table, with a setting for one. There was a note from Dad which said that he'd popped into town with his mother and that he'd be back around eleven.

I had a quick stroll around the kitchen, had a look out of the window and satisfied myself that there was nobody else around. I sat quickly down at the old wooden table and began to devour the milk, bread and jam as if I hadn't eaten for a week. The bread and jam were like nothing I had ever tasted before, it was absolutely wonderful. It must have been at least half a loaf that they had left for me, and after I'd polished it off, I was only sorry that there wasn't another half there because I'd have eaten that too.

Satisfied, not to mention slightly stuffed, I got up slowly, stretched and farted. Loudly. In that huge kitchen with the high ceiling and hard floor, it echoed like a fire cracker.

'Get in!' I said out loud and punched the air laughing.

At that point, I heard a muffled laugh, only to swing round and see Elsa, the old maid, washing some clothes in the washroom that backed on to the side of the kitchen that I hadn't noticed earlier. 'Oh my God,' I thought as I realised that she'd been there all along and seen and heard my fart extravaganza in all its glory! I was mortified. Embarrassed, I quickly scuttled over the floor and out of the swinging door, and headed behind the farmhouse, around the corner and straight into the first building I could see – one of the old barns – to hide and hopefully, die from the embarrassment.

Once in there, and free of my shame, it took a moment or two for my eyes to get used to the lack of light. When they did and I looked around me, I was amazed to see an Aladdin's cave of farm equipment and historic agricultural memorabilia displayed all throughout the barn. Everywhere I looked there was something either stacked in a pile, hanging on the wall, or suspended from the ceiling ….it was amazing. There were ploughs, horse brasses, bridles, chisels, rakes, hoes, engine parts, wheels, tyres and horseshoes. And much, much more. It took me ages to wander around the whole barn and take in the enormity of my find. Right above my head, suspended from the high ceiling was an old wicker basket for a hot air balloon, complete with its burners. I was amazed. I just walked around, touching everything, noticing the different smell of things and just totally absorbing this wondrous cave of possessions. It was like a museum of farming implements and associated tools throughout the 20th Century. At one point, I just leant against a wall to try to take it all in and decide what I next wanted to look closely at and inspect. Alongside me was a tarpaulin covering an object that I couldn't easily make out. As I shifted my balance to have a better look, I caught my foot on the edge of a plough, stumbled forward before bumping into it and making it crash to the floor.

And then I saw it.

I knew instantly what I'd just clumsily knocked over and my heart just stopped. It was absolutely beautiful, one of the most fantastic things I'd ever seen.

It was a professional racing bike.

I knew instantly it was a pro bike because the name emblazoned all over its frame was Carrera, who I recognised as a team from the Tour de France from many years ago.

I had no idea it why this fantastic bike would be there in my grandfather's barn amongst all that farming memorabilia, but I was absolutely chuffed that it was. I stood it up and supported it at arm's length, before crouching down and taking in its full beauty and shape. It was in immaculate condition, even the tyres were pumped up and hard, but then I noticed just above the two gear levers on the tube, that some of the blue and white paint design on the frame had been scraped off down to the metal, for a length of about two inches. Next to this bare metal remained the Italian flag which was untouched. I knew instantly what this was. A couple of years earlier, I'd seen a documentary on TV about Big Mig, where a camera crew spent a season with him and followed him all around, during his training, back to his home and then finally when he was competing on the roads, hills and mountains of Europe. One thing that stuck in my mind from the documentary was the moment when he took delivery of his new bikes at the beginning of the year, just as he was starting his training. What caught my eye was that each one had his name painted on the tube in a type of design that made it look like a signature, and right next to it was the Spanish flag. It was one of the classiest things I'd ever seen and I knew right there and then while I watched him joking with one of his team-mates about how cool his new bike looked, that one day, I too was going to have a pro bike with my own name – Daniel Williams – and the Welsh Flag next to it on the frame of my own pro-racing bike.

But there I was, aged 14, in a bizarre memorabilia laden barn in Northern Italy on the holiday from hell, but with one of those very bikes right in front of me.

I knew instantly that there was only one thing I was going to do.

After quickly testing the brakes, I was out of the barn, pushing the bike over the gravel until I was on the tarmac lane that led away from the farmhouse to one of the many country lanes that ran around the farm's borders. The bike was slightly too big for me – not much – but as I got used to it underneath me, I realised that it wasn't a full size adults bike, but more like a three quarter frame that some of the older teenagers in Three Crosses had when they sometimes passed me and Jamie in the Cilonen lanes.

This bike was special though, I knew that, I just floated along on it. The gears were so smooth, not clunky and rough like my five year old Raleigh that my mum had got from Halfords for me one

Christmas. It felt so light that it seemed to fly along at speeds that I usually had to put so much more effort in to achieve. This wasn't a new bike though. The style of the gears and pedals were even older than my Raleigh at home and the saddle was one of those old real leather ones with the studs in the back, that they must have used back in the 70s or 80s, but God it was in absolutely perfect condition and it was so comfortable. I'd never felt so at one with a bike in my life. I looked ahead and saw there was a left turn coming up that appeared to take me behind the farm and in the direction of the lanes I had seen that group of cyclists the previous evening from my bedroom window. I reached the left turn in no time, and as I straightened up after taking the bend, I saw that up ahead the road began to fall away after about a quarter of a mile into a slight dip before it rose up into a small hill which seemed to climb for a further five hundred yards or so from the bottom of the dip.

I knew what I had to do.

I changed up through all the gears until I really felt the resistance increase against my legs and after initially seeming to slow, I started to pick up some real speed. The further I went toward the point where the road began to slip away, the quicker my legs spun round and the faster I got, then, as the road dived away beneath me, I was down it in a flash. Almost as soon as I sped down its slope, quickly it started to rise. The speed I was carrying though just threw me straight up the opposite slope, so much so that I didn't need to change gear until I got about halfway up it. As the steepness of this small hill then quickly kicked in, I went down through a couple of the gears as smooth as I had ever experienced, and made it up the hill easily until I was back up onto a flat stretch of road from which – to my left – I could see the back of the farmhouse and the outbuildings. The other thing I could see clearly was the huge cypress tree, under which my grandfather had been standing the previous afternoon. Just as I turned back to focus on the straight empty road ahead of me, something glinted from beneath that big tree. I quickly looked back again, and there he was. My grandfather. I couldn't make out his face, but I could just about make out his form in the shadows, the glint coming occasionally off his pocket watch that he wore dangling from the buttons of his dark grey waistcoat. I realised that I was too far away for him to know that it was me, because the only reason that I knew it was him was that I knew that's where he liked to stand and the clue given from his pocket watch. But surely from that distance he would have had no idea that it was me out speeding along the road on a bike taken from his very own barn? He probably thought I was still tucked away in my bedroom. Nevertheless, a slight guilty conscience kicked in to the front of my mind for the briefest of moments and part of me thought I ought to turn back. I realised that whether or not he knew it was me at that precise moment, he would definitely find out soon enough. I also understood that even if he didn't give me a row, my father certainly would as soon as he knew my bad behaviour in front of his family had now progressed to include pinching a bike and taking part in his hated cycling. Then, just as my guilty conscience was about to get the better of me, I remembered a phrase Jamie's dad had explained to us both one day when he'd had a row off Jamie's mother for staying out all night after a Wales v New Zealand rugby match.

'The thing is boys, when I knew I was over an hour late, I knew she'd give me a big bollocking anyway, that's when I thought I may as well stay out 'till the bitter end with the lads ... may as well be hung for a sheep as well as a lamb.'

Jamie's dad was always coming out with weird phrases like that, always laughing as he said them. I laughed out loud thinking about it and guilty conscience banished, as I continued speeding along this perfect, deserted road under an already hot mid-morning sun, I started laughing aloud and shouting at the top of my voice 'I may as well be hung for a sheep as well as a lamb' which I repeated constantly for about five hundred yards as I began pedaling with all my strength.

The feeling of warmth from the sun on my face combined with the coolness of the breeze flowing through my hair, not to mention my insane shouting of wise old sayings, made me reflect for a moment that I was as happy as I'd been in a very, very long time. I felt so free. Cycling always had this effect on me.

After about half an hour when the road had begun to meander a bit, and the farmhouse now long out of sight, I remembered the harsh lesson I'd learned from my ill-fated trip to Port Eynon with Jamie all those years before. I realised I now had quite a way to get back, and as I hadn't filled up on pop and chocolate, figured that I had better turn and head for home. I braked gently, slowed, made sure there were no cars, then went down the gears again before slowly swinging the bike round in a tight 180, making sure I didn't topple into the ditch that edged the left hand side of the road. Within moments, I was back up to speed with the slight breeze now behind me, helping, crouching as low as I could to the red taped drop handlebars and hurtling back along the road. Soon, I arrived back at the point where the hill I had climbed earlier would now drop me back down at huge speed before finally turning right at the end of the road and eventually back to the farm. As I approached the rear of the farm after a period of intense pedaling that felt as easy as I'd ever experienced on a bike, I saw the glint again come from near the huge cypress tree and, not surprisingly, there he was. Definitely watching this time, my grandfather was standing well away from the tree, out in the open – with a pair of binoculars ... aimed at me!

Shite.

I slowed for a moment, then I thought of Jamie's dad again and laughed. 'Sheep as a lamb' I thought to myself and sniggered. Right, if he wants a show he can have one, I thought. I picked up the speed again, got to the right gear, crouched as low as I could, leaning further forward this time, in front of the handlebars, until my head was actually right over the thin, slick front tyre. Then, I kicked for all I was worth. God that bike was good. It responded to my increase in energy and just flew. Suddenly, the feeling I had, of the effort being transferred down onto the road by the wonderful machinery of the bike, was the most exhilarating sensation in the world. Just at the brow of the hill, before I was about to disappear from view of the farm, and more importantly my grandfather's binoculars, I gave the briefest of glances over my right shoulder. He was there still, peering through those glasses. My grandfather, watching every move I was making. But then I was gone, piling down the hill as fast as I'd ever been on a bike in my life before.

12

*

I SLOWLY brought the bike to a halt on the tarmac lane that led to the gravel driveway that I'd pushed the bike over about an hour before. I dismounted and half carried and half pushed it, trying not to make too much noise on the loose stones as I secretly tried to make it back to the barn unseen.

One bonus I spotted – Dad's hire Bravo was not there which meant he was still out with his mother. At least there'd be some time to enjoy my moment of freedom on that fantastic bike before the inevitable row came from his lips, I thought. Quickly, I made it to the barn unchallenged, wheeled the bike over to the tarpaulin, which I'd left strewn across the sawdust covered floor when I left earlier. As I took one last, longing look at the bike before I put it back under wraps, my eyes soon focused back to the piece of bare metal next to the untouched Italian flag. I gently rolled my finger over it, feeling the rough edges of the broken paint, flaking slightly as my fingertip rubbed it.

'Whose name used to be on here?' I whispered to myself. It was obviously a pro cyclist, but I didn't know of any famous Italian cyclists other than 'The Pirate' Pantani, only the many French, Belgian and Dutch professionals, and of course Big Mig and his Spanish mates. I wonder who this bike belonged to, I pondered quietly.

'Did you enjoy that?' came a deep rich Italian voice from the darkness at the back of the barn, which made me jump higher than my dad had made me the night before when he crept up on me in the bedroom. Nearly dropping the bike, I grabbed it, steadied it and then carried on pulling the tarpaulin over it, ignoring the voice.

'Let me give you a hand with that my boy,' said my grandfather in heavily accented, yet surprisingly, almost perfect English, as he walked toward me from the back of the barn, his pocket watch still catching the odd ray of light that was forcing itself through the dusty, cracked window high above me.

In normal circumstances I would have said sorry straight away for taking it without asking, but I knew I couldn't forget my mission which was to be as unapproachable as possible to everyone, so that I could get away from Italy as soon as I could. So instead, I just pulled the tarpaulin down all around the bike until it could no longer be seen, and leant it back against the wall of the barn, just as I had found it.

'Nice bike Danilo, no?' said my grandfather.

I turned to leave without saying anything, but as I did so, a strong hand placed itself gently yet firmly on my shoulder. The touch of his hand said everything. It was firm enough to show that I wasn't being allowed to leave yet, but soft enough to say that here was someone who was caring and gentle, and didn't want to frighten me.

'Come Danilo, come. I have prepared some lemonade. It is only you and I ... oh and of course Elsa, the maid. But I think you know she is here don't you?' And with that, cackling with laughter, he walked out of the barn to the kitchen.

My brain was so frazzled at that point I didn't know what he meant about Elsa and why he was laughing, then I remembered. The fart. Shit. Still, it brought a quick, embarrassed, smile to my face.

Dawdling slightly, I followed my grandfather and finally made it to the back door, only to meet him coming back out carrying a tray, two large glasses with Campari stamped on them, and a tall bottle of cloudy lemonade.

'It is too nice to sit inside, let us go down to the stream and drink there.'

Soon, we were sitting on some thick old logs that had been hollowed out in places to resemble seats. The logs were situated by the edge of a stream, and there I sat, in silence, awaiting the telling off that was certain to follow.

'Nice lemonade, boy?' asked my grandfather with a toothy grin, made up of wonky yellowing teeth and a big gap in the middle where one was missing, which gave his smile an almost cartoon look.

I just nodded.

'Good, good.' He paused for a moment then spoke again. 'Ok. In case you do not know, I am your grandfather, Umberto. I am the father of your father Gianluca, and also head of this family, here in Cassano Spinola. I was born in that house,' he said, casually pointing over his shoulder, 'As was my father and his father before him. Our family is an honest one, a hardworking one, and we have always earned our money from the land.'

Again, I feigned disinterest, content instead to look into the deepest part of the dark stream moving slowly before me. I wondered how come he spoke such good English, yet his wife spoke hardly any, but I certainly wasn't going to ask him a question like that, I didn't want to show any interest in him or his family at all.

'The road you were on is perfect for cycling, no?' he asked me. 'It is where I saw *Il Campionissimo* for the first time when I was a young man, just after the war.'

Il Campionissimo? I thought, what the hell is that ... a circus?

My grandfather sat there a moment, lemonade glass in hand, staring out toward the road I'd been flying along just half an hour earlier, lost in a haze of memories. They must have been happy, because all the time he was gazing out in silence, he looked so content, with a simple smile on his face. While he was lost in his thoughts, it gave me the first opportunity to really have a close look at this man who, biologically anyway, was so close to me. Just looking at him, you could instantly tell that here was a very fit man. It was hard to put an age on him, because his skin was so tanned and taut that it probably helped to hide how old he really was, but I guessed him to be at least in his mid-60s, possibly even older. His old fashioned pin striped shirt sleeves were rolled up to the elbow to expose the most fascinating part of him – his arms. They were incredible. I looked down at my puny, white forearms with girl's wrists, then glanced forlornly back at his. His wrists were as wide as a small branch of an oak tree. These thick wrists led up to forearms that were like Vin Diesel's. They were immensely muscled and toned, almost the arms you would expect to see on an athlete. As I was giving him the once-over, he caught me looking and laughed.

'A lot of hard work went in to building these,' He said rubbing his forearms up and down, before reaching forward and grabbing my left arm. Then, he held it up to the sky as if he was examining it, rotating it slowly and laughing 'Not too bad my boy, you are developing well. How old are you now?'

'Fourteen' I replied, just managing to suppress a smile, remembering that I was trying to remain aloof.

'Fourteen? Fourteen?' he exclaimed with delight. 'Goodness, in no time at all you will soon be pulling up tree trunks when we get you eating some good Italian pasta,' laughing loudly at his own joke as he let my arm drop back into my lap.

'Now then. Tell me about you Danilo. I know not much of you because your father has been away so long. I still have photos of you of course, sent to me by your lovely mother. How is she?'

'You know my mother?' I asked. 'How?' My mother had always told me that she'd never been to Italy, so how did he know her?

'Well, I've never met your mother my boy, which I'm quite sad about. But ever since you were born, your mother has written to me and your grandmother telling us about you and sending us all those lovely photos as you have been growing up. She even sends them since my son and she sadly split up.' He stopped at this point looking genuinely sad.

'I had no idea.' I said with some surprise, and feeling oddly proud of my mum's actions.

'Yes, thanks to your mother, I knew what you looked like before you even came here. I have photographs of you in your father's arms, in your Christmas Nativity play as the Shepherd,' I blushed at this awful memory, 'and in your football kit – Swansea City – are they any good? I bet they wouldn't beat any Italian teams' he laughed.

'What do you mean?' I said smiling 'We've got some good players,' I said.

'There's only one Welsh player who would get in any Italian teams I have seen, and that was John Charles. He too was from Swansea. Have you heard of him?'

'I think so,' I said. 'But I don't know much about him.'

'He was magnificent. He was the best player for 'The Old Lady' – do you know who they are?'

'I think so' I said, 'It's Juventus isn't it?'

'Good boy Danilo!' my grandfather exploded with glee 'Good boy.' he repeated 'You follow your grandfather – you are a very clever boy!' This remark drew another big belly laugh from him, exposing his crooked teeth again as he threw his head back laughing, which in turn made me laugh.

'That's better, it's so good to see you laugh, you are a beautiful boy when you smile, you should do it more often.'

As I blushed and avoided his eyes, I knew that my plan to be as grumpy as possible while I was in Italy was now doomed, and it was largely due to this funny, happy man who seemed to fill the air around me with good feelings and happiness. He was my grandfather. I realised it at that precise moment how important that was. I also realised that I loved him instantly.

Just as my brain was trying to make sense of the events of the morning and recognising that there were so many questions I needed to ask this man, starting with how he spoke such good English, I heard that familiar crush of tyres over gravel, and looked back to the house to see my father pulling up in front of the barn with my grandmother.

I looked straight at my grandfather, who quickly lost that look of joy and happiness in eyes.

'Go to him now,' he said gripping my shoulder ever so slightly, 'and keep the ride on the bike as our little secret for now, eh?'

'Oh, you know he hates cycling too?'

My grandfather paused slightly, before continuing. 'Sadly boy, I do. I do.' There was something in his eyes that begged a question from me, but with a wave of his powerful arms, he sent me on my way to see my dad and grandmother. I'd gone about five yards when he called after me.

'Danilo – be a good boy for your father. He is a good honourable man who is troubled. He could do with your beautiful smile more often.'

I thought for a minute, looked at this lovely old man and nodded.

'Ok.' And off I went to see Dad and my grandmother.

'And another thing,' he called. 'You can call me Grandpa from now on, no?'

'Ok, Grandpa,' I smiled.

The rest of the day was pretty uneventful, but one thing had changed, I had made my mind up to speak to Dad when we got to our bedrooms, to sort of say sorry and just try to make the peace. My plan to remain obnoxious now seemed pointless, especially as I'd so instantly fallen in love with my grandfather. However, when my father caught up with me in the lounge after tea, it quickly all changed back to how it had been before my chat with my grandfather.

'Have you had a nice day?' he started.

'Yes, thanks' I smiled.

'That's good. What did you get up to?'

'Well, I had a long chat with Grandpa and we talked about a footballer called John Charles from Swansea who played for Juventus.' Dad's own smile immediately slid off his face, followed by a tut, as he rolled his eyes to the heavens in disapproval.

The anger rose in me straight away.

'What's wrong with you, Dad?' I exclaimed. 'As soon as I mention sport you become a different person. Just because you hate it, because you've probably never been any good at it, don't take it out on me, it's not my fault. I am good and I love it. So there. You'd better get used to it. Grandpa loves sport, I can tell that straight away, so why don't you?' And with that, I jumped up and left the room, furious with my father once again. As I left, I caught the disapproving look of my grandmother who then looked sadly at my father. As I went to climb the stairs, my grandfather came out of the kitchen, carrying a large glass of red wine and some cheese on a small plate.

'I tried Grandpa, I really did. He's just not like us, he hates sport.'

My grandfather sighed, motioned me up the stairs, turned and went back into the kitchen, shoulders sagging. Within half an hour I was asleep dreaming dreams of cycling through this beautiful part of Italy, me in the middle on my new pro bike, with my name and Welsh flag on the tube and Big Mig on one side of me and Jan Ullrich on the other. I was so happy, I didn't want it to ever end.

13

✻

DAD shook me gently awake in the morning. 'I have to go to Torino today and I will be gone until tonight. Your grandmother will look after you. I will see you later. Please be a good boy.' After a brief pause he said 'and don't take your annoyance with me out on them, they are good people.' I just shrugged and rolled back over and pretended to go back to sleep. I heard him quietly close the door behind him.

I lay there for about ten minutes, just taking in the sunlight creeping through the gaps in the curtains, and wondering what the day had in store for me.

After another fantastic breakfast, this time in the company of my grandmother who spoke throughout in Italian apart from the odd phrase of English, where she always mixed up her words, the best being 'Danilo, when today you are thirsty, the fridge will have for you cock and cola.' I nearly choked on my bread and jam at that point.

After breakfast, I noticed I hadn't seen my grandfather since I'd got up. I strolled outside and had a look in the garden. No sign. I walked around the side of the house to see if he was out at the front. As I got there, the scene that greeted me filled me with joy. There, leaning against the old water fountain in the middle of the courtyard was the bike I'd sneaked out the day before, this time with two water bottles – full – attached to the frame which weren't there yesterday. As I walked toward it, I heard that familiar voice coming out from within the barn.

'Danilo, today we ride.' What greeted me emerging from the barn stopped me in my tracks. There, pushing out a racing bike that looked as though it was fifty years old was my grandfather. Grinning. Then, when I got full sight of him, it was my turn to grin. Instead of his usually scruffy dark grey trousers and waistcoat, he was dressed, head to toe, in, well, beige.

I couldn't stop my laughter.

On his feet were little black slippers, made of leather, and pulled tight with thick black laces. They looked about two sizes too small for him. Then, he had thick woollen socks with a pattern of light and dark beige diamonds. Tucked into these were thick corduroy trousers – again in beige. Despite it being yet another lovely sunny morning, he wore a thick woollen jumper with a zip to the neck, around which he had wrapped a handkerchief-cum-scarf ... again, all beige. All this was topped off with a black beret and thick, dark sunglasses.

'Hey, why you laugh?' he said in mock anger. 'This was my best riding gear from when I was a young man!' before bursting out laughing himself. 'Come, you go and get changed and we'll go before the rain comes.'

Rain? I looked around and couldn't see a cloud in the sky ... I laughed again at this mad old man who I was now so delighted to have as my grandfather.

Within twenty minutes, the pair of us were cycling gently along a flat road that ran the opposite way to the route I'd taken the day before. I didn't want to go too fast because of my grandfather's age, but after this opening section, he wasn't even breathing heavily.

'Grandpa, do you cycle often?'

'My boy, the last time this old Italian backside sat on a bike was about twenty years ago. Today, with you, I experience once again the joy of cycling on an open road ... the joy of my life. I have you to thank for this.'

'Why me Grandpa?' I asked

'Because yesterday, when I saw your face as you uncovered that bike, and you took in the beauty of what is a truly fantastic machine, you reminded me of the time when I had my first racing bike, at a time when the World was still at war, and our country, Italy, was totally bust. To me, the bike represented a chance of a life away from the poverty we were experiencing and the possibilities and freedom it offered me were endless. There have been times in my life when I have forgotten that simple dream, but yesterday, in your face, I saw it again, Danilo.'

For the next hour we cycled, me asking my grandfather lots of questions about Italy and my family, trying to fill in as many gaps as possible about this family I never knew I had. One of the questions I had for him was how he came to speak perfect English. He brushed the answer aside saying it was just 'the war' and he would explain it all to me 'one day.' I didn't feel I knew him well enough to pry any further, but sensed that there was more that he wanted to tell me about that than he was letting on. Despite this, there was much laughter – especially when we stopped at a bend in the road and he told me about the time when he came to that very spot when he was about fifteen and because he was looking down trying to free a part of his trousers from the chain, he missed the turn and ploughed straight into the side of a cow eating grass on the verge, totally buckling his wheel and sending him cart-wheeling over the cow's back and ending up in a pile of its shit that it had just freshly deposited on the ground. He laughed for about five minutes as he told me that tale, and it was impossible not to laugh with him. But, amongst the laughter, there was also sadness, especially when he explained how his father – my great-grandfather – was taken away one day by the Germans in the early part of the War. Apparently, my great-grandfather was quite outspoken locally about the way that the Italians had become allies of the Germans, and he had been warned a few times by people in Cassano Spinola that he had better be more careful of speaking so openly about his opposition to the Germans. Eventually, because he wouldn't co-operate with the Fascists who were now, along with the rest of Italy, running the area of Piedmont where they lived, my great-grandfather started to receive threats. But, according to my grandfather, he refused to be bullied by these fascists and still refused to co-operate, or perhaps more importantly, keep quiet. Then, when a division of Germans were posted to the surrounding area of Cassano Spinola, and began using the town as though it was their own, my great-grandfather apparently complained to the local council that they should not be allowed to use the shops and bars of the town. This must have been the final straw. My grandfather solemnly told me how he remembered the noise of a German military truck on the gravel driveway early one morning, followed by the sound of boots crunching over the ground, and shouting until the soldiers finally found my great-grandfather. He then told me how he witnessed these Germans arresting his father, and dumping him onto the back of their truck. Running out of the farmhouse with a pitchfork and screaming at the Germans for them to stop, my grandfather was hit across the head by a rifle butt, leaving him on the floor, bleeding, to watch helplessly as his father was taken away. He never, ever saw him again. My grandfather was just a teenager at the time. He showed me the big scar on the side of his head and told me that from that day – along with his brother Claudio – they had to run the farm together for the sake of their mother. Cycling, he admitted, was the only thing that gave him hope, so he cycled as often, and as far and as fast, as he could. It was the only way he could deal with his anger.

'It was that anger I saw in you yesterday, when you flew down that road behind the house and I watched you from behind the tree,' he told me. 'To have the anger is not a bad thing. But a beautiful thing is to use the anger correctly and to take it out on the road ... not the bike ... the road, that is important Danilo. The bike is your best friend, it is the road that is your enemy.'

By late morning we stopped and ate the food that my grandfather had stuffed inside loads of hidden pockets in his beige cardigan.

'Lack of fuel is the cyclist's biggest curse. Without it, you will have the same effect as running a Ferrari on fumes ... nothing but worry and a long walk home. To learn to cycle, you must first learn to eat, that is why I give you the huge breakfast of milk, bread and jam. That burns slowly in your gut until you need to top it up now'.

So, there we sat, feasting on chocolate, raisins, olives, sandwiches of bread and jam along with the bottles of water. Plenty of water.

'Fluid to a cyclist, is like oil to an engine. Without it….*Kaboom*!' and my grandfather laughed as he impersonated an explosion.

As I rested after our re-fueling pit stop, I again looked at the sun in the clear blue sky and felt as happy and content as I ever had. What had started out as possibly being the worst three weeks of my life was surprisingly starting to become something so much different.

'Come Danilo, the rain,' said my grandfather, urging me to get back onto the bike and pointing to the sky.

I just laughed as I motioned to a cloudless sky, and just played along with what must have been one of his games.

'For me, the ride home will be leisurely. For you, it will be quicker. I want to watch you because from what I have seen of you, I think you can be good. So you go, leave me behind, and I'll look at you to see if you can become a champion. But,' he warned me, 'don't go out too fast, this route takes more energy than you may think. And remember the rain. That is the opponent you have to beat today. If you ride correctly you will beat him.'

So, still confused by his continued references to the rain on such a stunningly beautiful day, off I went, and as much as I loved my grandfather and thanked him for the advice, there was no way that I was going to take it easy. I went off like a bullet. If you want to see whether I can become a champion, I thought to myself, then let's see if you can keep up with this.

After an hour, I was really struggling.

Because we'd done the route out from the farm at such a leisurely pace, I hadn't noticed how far we'd actually gone. For the first forty odd minutes on the flat road back, I'd gone as quick as my legs could manage and felt absolutely fantastic, and the few times I'd glanced back, my grandfather had become smaller and smaller in the distance. But in the last twenty minutes, my legs had become heavier, especially the fronts of my thighs which had begun to ache considerably. Still, it couldn't be that far now I remember thinking and I peered ahead, hoping to spot a landmark that would show me where the farmhouse was.

After another five or so minutes, I saw the farm on the horizon, and despite the pain in my legs starting to border on the edge of cramp, I was still managing to keep going, but at a much slower pace than before.

Then, one of the loudest cracks of thunder I'd ever heard in my life exploded up above me, absolutely frightening the life out of me. Unbelievably, the blue sky had begun to change to black before my very eyes, and my enemy, the rain, was certainly not far away. How on earth had my grandfather known that?

I kicked into my pedals to generate some speed, but there was nothing there, except the flare-up of cramp that attacked my left calf. I took my foot out of the toe clip to stretch the cramped up muscle, which helped slightly, but pedaling with one leg, severely reduced my speed. I got off, stretched and managed to free the muscle from the cramp, but when I got back on, the cramp returned instantly and I was basically only able to limp home and hope I'd manage to beat the rain.

Then came another enormous crack of thunder.

Thankfully, up ahead, the farmhouse was growing in size, surely only a mile or so to go. But then, another noise from behind. A kind of whirring and whistling – a car? We hadn't seen one all day. I pulled to the right slightly and looked behind me. The whirring was the chain of a bike, the whistling came from an old man dressed completely in beige with a black beret, and sunglasses.

As he just effortlessly overtook me, my grandfather motioned to the heavens: 'The rain Danilo, the rain ... don't let him beat you,' and off he went, leaving me as if I was a marathon runner trying to outpace a sprinter. All he left behind for me was his laughter as he went.

As I finally pulled into the drive and made my way to the barn, I was absolutely soaked to the skin. The downpour that I'd cycled through for the previous five minutes was the heaviest I'd ever experienced. It was like being in the middle of one of those nature programmes on TV that feature freakish weather and storms. And there, under the shelter of the entrance of the barn, leaned my grandfather, sipping some lemonade and laughing.

'Today you learned the most important lesson. Speed is not everything. In fact, sometimes it is nothing at all. The fastest man will not win every race, in fact he loses most. But the man that understands his distance and his capabilities will usually be the man to beat. Think about that – this is something you must learn, pace yourself, it is incredibly important that you understand that. Now Danilo, give me that bike and go and get a bath ... my son would kill me if he found out about this, so remember to keep it our secret,' and he smiled as he took the bike off me and whisked it into the garage, while I limped slowly across the gravel, through the rain and up to the hot bath that awaited.

14

I WAS so tired, I fell asleep almost straight away in that lovely, hot bath, and only woke quite a while later when the coldness of the water brought me round. Shivering, I got out, and realised instantly that I'd forgotten to bring a towel in with me. I had a quick look around and saw a cupboard, so I opened it and had a look inside. The cupboard was massive and was packed with white towels piled on the wooden slatted shelves. As I reached up for one of the towels, I shifted my weight, and a splinter from the wooden floor nicked my foot, and I stumbled forward in pain. As I put my hand out to regain my balance, my eyes were diverted to the floor near the back of the cupboard, and I saw what looked like a massive, old, leather trunk, with what appeared to be an Italian flag and the worn image of a bicycle painted underneath it.

Once I'd removed the splinter and was dry and warm, I couldn't resist the urge to have a peek inside the trunk in the cupboard.

In retrospect, I know I shouldn't have because it was quite a nosy thing to do, but it just seemed to beckon me toward it to have a look, especially when I looked at the flag and bicycle again. It was so old, antique looking and mysterious, I really couldn't help myself. I can't explain the feeling I had as I pulled it towards me, it was a combination of guilt and excitement, but I just knew that inside it would be something special. However, when I flipped its lid open, the contents still managed to take my breath away.

It was obvious that the trunk hadn't been opened for ages – years even – because of the dust all around it on the floor which scattered when I'd pulled it forward, not to mention the dust that fell from the lid when I opened it. The trunk's contents were like a museum exhibit of professional cycling. Anything that you would have used if you had been a professional cyclist years and years ago was inside. There were old cycling shirts, not made of lycra with zips like the modern ones, but made of wool with large buttons, huge, drooping pointed collars and pockets on the chest, which I assumed were for keeping food. All the shirts were in perfect condition and absolutely beautiful, mainly a pale blue all over, apart from a white band around the chest that, had a sponsor's name on the front and back, all in capital letters – BIANCHI. One of the shirts, in smaller letters underneath the BIANCHI logo, had another sponsor's logo – Pirelli. I'd heard of them, they were a tyre company, but I hadn't ever heard of Bianchi. Underneath the shirts were a few pairs of black cycling shorts, again not made of lycra, but some older material that I wasn't familiar with. These also had the words BIANCHI on both legs, in white capital letters stitched individually onto the black material. They looked so authentic when compared to the modern kit I was used to which was all pre-printed transfers instead of these beautifully stitched logos.

For a while, I simply sat on the floor in front of the cupboard holding these fantastic items in front of me. I just knew they were professional cycling jerseys and shorts from long ago – but why were they here? They obviously weren't my father's – he hated cycling, and my grandfather had been a farmer all his life, so they weren't his either. So whose were they? Was there a family member I hadn't met or heard about? I remember my grandfather had spoken about his brother Claudio, perhaps it all belonged to him. I decided that if I rooted around in the trunk a bit more, I might find some clues as to who all the kit belonged to. I put the jerseys down and continued sifting through the treasure trove, captivated. There were several pairs of cycling gloves, which seemed to have leather palms but then appeared to be made of string for the backs of the hand. Then there were several old fashioned leather helmets that looked more like rugby scrum caps, a few pairs of socks and tiny cycling caps, those odd looking ones with tiny up-turned peaks, again blue and white, with the BIANCHI logo across the front. Underneath all this fantastic kit were lots of old newspapers and scrap books. Everything was in

Italian, but every headline and story beneath contained somewhere the same name – 'Fausto Coppi'. Most of the newspapers were made of pink paper and were called *La Gazetto dello Sport*. I tried to read one of the big headlines which said 'Fausto Coppi – Ancora un altro magnifico vittoria'. I didn't know what it said but I guessed that 'magnifico' meant 'magnificent', but whatever it said, the way the headline sat so bold against this beautiful pink paper, it looked better than any sporting headline I'd ever seen before. There were so many newspapers that featured 'Coppi' as the headline, but one simply said *Il Campionissimo*.

I thought about that for a moment, *Il Campionissimo*? Wasn't that something my grandfather had said the other day? I was certain it was. No matter, I spent the next five minutes looking through the newspapers and scrap books – there were at least ten of those – and they all seemed devoted to this man Coppi. He was obviously a brilliant cyclist as there were so many pictures of him holding the winning trophies, getting presented with gold sashes and loads of other prizes. But why was there such a collection of his cycling memorabilia in this trunk? Was he a relative of the family? He had a different surname of course, so maybe that ruled that idea out. Unless, perhaps he was Grandma's brother, it may have been that her maiden name had been Coppi. It would also explain the old bike that Granddad had ridden the other day – it must have been this bloke Coppi's. Also, what was that phrase *Il Campionissimo* all about? It was obviously important because it appeared in the scrapbooks plenty of times. But what did it mean? There was only one person I could ask to answer all my questions.

My grandfather.

But now I had a problem. My father and grandfather, who had hardly spoken a word to each other since we'd arrived, were never in the same room together, they avoided each other totally. Despite me being totally horrible to my father, he never left me alone when he was around, because – apart from my grandfather – nobody else really spoke English that I could understand, so he was always nearby to translate. I also had the additional problem, that even if my grandfather was in the next room, he'd made me promise that I wasn't to mention our bike trips or cycling in general in front of my father. All these issues meant that I could only talk to my grandfather about the trunk when my father was not around. There was nothing for it, I would have to wait.

And the suspense was already killing me.

The next day my father decided he would do me a favour, and decided to spend the day with me. Even though my hard stance toward him was thawing thanks to the nice things my grandfather had told me about him, I struggled to hide my disappointment that I would not now be seeing my grandfather for at least another day, which meant another 24 hours before I could quiz him about this Fausto Coppi guy and his cycling gear that filled the trunk.

Surprisingly and against the odds, Dad and me had quite a nice day together. He took us to Alessandria, the main city of the area, and we bought some presents for Mum, Rob and of course Jamie. I bought him a Juventus T-shirt, it was black and white, so I knew he could also wear it when we watched Swansea City too. In the late afternoon, Dad took us to a café on the corner of the square, he had a coffee and I had the biggest ice cream I'd ever seen. The sun was out, there was music playing and Dad looked as happy as I think I'd ever seen him, just sitting there watching the world go by as we sat on the edge of the hectic town square.

'Did you come here when you were a boy, Dad?' I asked.

'Yes, very often,' he replied. 'Most Saturdays when I was a bit younger than you are now, I'd either get the bus in with my best friend Franco, or sometimes, Papa would bring us in his wagon. I've always loved this square. It's always been busy like this with plenty of people and lots of different noises. Franco and I would sit over there,' he smiled, pointing at the church on the opposite side of the square, 'and we'd stuff ourselves with ice creams like the one you've got there. They were great days.'

I realised that this was the first time that my father had ever told me anything about his childhood and the look on his face showed that he'd obviously had some extremely happy times at this place. So there we sat for about an hour or so, chatting about nothing in particular, but just getting to know each other a little better, like every father and son should do. I loved the normality of it.

By then, our afternoon together had gone so well and we were so relaxed, that I felt I could ask him a question. I wasn't going to break my promise to Grandpa and mention the cycling nor was I going to admit to snooping around in the chest looking at the cycling stuff. But I didn't think it would do any harm if I did a little research.

'Dad?' I started.

'Yes, Danilo.'

'Who's Fausto Coppi?'

His face changed immediately. Gone was the relaxed smile of the past hour or so and back instantly was the fixed, taut frown I'd known for the past four or five years.

'Who on earth has told you his name?' He barked, just about containing his anger.

I blushed immediately and stumbled over my response.

'Um, oh, nobody. I, er, just saw a picture of him in one of the shops earlier, he looked like a cyclist that's all and you know I like cycling.'

The quizzical way he looked at me suggested that he just about believed me, but clearly, had his doubts. I was thankful once again to Jamie's dad. One day, when he was explaining to us that it was ok to tell the odd lie – as long as nobody was hurt by it – he said that the very best lies actually have some truth in them. Anyway, it seemed to have worked, but the very mention of Coppi's name seemed to upset Dad greatly.

'He was a cyclist and I hate him. Let's just leave it at that,' he said, 'and please don't mention his name to me again. Come on, it's time we were getting back, Grandma will be preparing our food.'

And with that, it was over. Dad was back to his normal grumpy self, I was back to my normal annoyed self and all I wanted to do was speak to Granddad about this Fausto Coppi bloke and why my father hated him so much. As we drove back in the Bravo, again in silence, I couldn't wait until I was alone with Granddad again so I could finally get to the bottom of this mystery; I just had to find out.

15

✳

THE next day, Dad and Grandma announced at breakfast that they were heading into the town for the morning and would I like to go with them? I'd been expecting something like this to happen. So, that morning when I'd got up, I pretended that I wasn't feeling well, and just as Dad was asking me if I wanted to join him and Grandma, I decided it was time for my condition to worsen. After some fussing by Grandma, it was decided that I wouldn't go as I obviously wasn't feeling too clever and I'd also helpfully suggested that I'd probably be sick in the car if I had to travel any sort of distance. My plan nearly backfired on me at one point because Grandma told Dad at one stage that she would stay behind and look after me and that he should go to town on his own, to which Dad replied that it was no problem to him if they'd cancel their trip for a day and go another time. Horrified, I quickly protested and said that I didn't want to spoil anyone's day and that Grandpa would be around so he'd be able to keep an eye on me if required, and that I'd just go up to bed and stay there anyway. Grandma called Grandpa in at this point and spoke to him so quickly in Italian, it was as if she'd turned into a human machine gun again, rattling off every syllable at such speed. I watched all the nods and glances between Dad, Grandma and Grandpa before it was all agreed, and then just ten minutes later, I was in my bedroom window waving weakly to them both as they took the lane away from the farm, turned right and headed off into town. Outstanding! Now, apart from Grandpa who was in one of the barns, I was all alone. There was only one thing for it.

The trunk.

I'd already decided that I wanted to have another good root around in it because I'd been interrupted by a noise outside the last time and, worried I'd get a row, had panicked and threw everything back in and pushed it all the way to the back of the cupboard, before leaving the bathroom to get changed. Now, all alone, I knew it was the perfect opportunity for me to have another look. After about ten minutes hanging around and keeping quiet, I crept into the bathroom and pulled the door a little behind me. Quietly, I soon had the trunk open and was carefully going back through its contents, trying to seek out things that I must have missed when I first had a rummage through it. Along with the other pieces of equipment, I now spotted some other treats like two pairs of cycling shoes – black – a couple of pairs of really expensive looking sunglasses and then, right at the bottom underneath the newspapers and scrapbooks and wrapped in some old tissue paper, I discovered the best item of all. As I unwrapped the tissue paper carefully and opened it out to display its contents, the item of clothing that was revealed almost took my breath away. It was an Italian National cycling jersey.

And it was absolutely stunning.

I sat there for what seemed an age, just holding this jersey up to the light, then against my own chest – it dwarfed me totally – and finally, I just lay it in my lap tracing my fingers over the rough sewn edges of the badge that stood proud from the material it was stitched to, right in the centre of the chest. The short sleeved jersey was Italian blue (obviously!), again had two front pockets on the chest like the Bianchi jerseys, but this time, instead of the buttons and clumsy collars of those light blue and white ones, it had a stylish zip from just above the chest pockets up to the neck. And instead of collars, the shirt just zipped up and met like the circular cut of an old fash-ioned granddad shirt. But what fascinated me most about this fantastic sporting jersey was its badge. There it sat proudly, right in the middle of the shirt, on top of the two pockets. About three inches long, it was in the shape of a shield and had a thick white vertical stripe down the middle of it, flanked by a green stripe on the left and a red one on the right. Above the colours, embroidered in gold capital letters along the top on a black background was one word; ITALIA.

It was magnificent.

Ever since I'd had my first ever Swansea City shirt as a kid, I'd become almost obsessed with sporting jerseys of any type. Thanks to my mum, I now owned several other Swansea City jerseys, a Swansea rugby club shirt along with my Welsh rugby and football shirts. I loved them all, but also knew that none of them were authentic originals, worn by the stars I idolised. Those were the shirts I really wanted, shirts worn by players and sportsmen of the highest level, shirts worn on the field of battle. And now, here I was, holding what I was certain to be a genuine international cycling jersey of the country of my father and grandfather – Italy. Right there and then at that precise moment, I felt my Italian heritage surge right through me like never before. I'd always tried to hide it in the past, actively avoiding connecting with it and it was only Jamie, of all my school-mates, who knew anything about my 'other name', but here, sitting in a bathroom in an old farmhouse in Piedmont, Italy, that land of my father's came surging right through me, directly via the shirt I was holding. Fausto Coppi's Italian cycling jersey ... whoever Fausto Coppi was. I felt hugely inspired and strangely elated. I couldn't have been happier.

'I see you have been snooping around, young Danilo.'

For the third time this week, I jumped right out of my skin, nearly hitting my head on the shelf that held all the towels.

'Grandpa,' I said as I swung round, desperately trying to cover up for myself, and thinking what best to say. 'I'm really sorry. I didn't mean to...' my words tailed off as he again raised one of his strong arms, and with a wave of his huge hand, stopped me speaking instantly.

'Let me have the shirt. Go downstairs and wait for me in the kitchen. We will talk.'

I handed him the shirt and saw the anger in his eyes as I walked out. I stopped for a moment and said simply: 'Sorry.'

He ignored me. I was gutted. Yet again.

As I walked down the long staircase that led to the kitchen, I knew I had done wrong, and was really angry with myself for doing it and above all, being caught by my grandfather. The sense of disappointment I felt in letting him down in this way was great, but in my heart I knew it was because I was young and so excited by what the trunk contained that I couldn't help myself – I would have to tell him that and hope that he would understand and forgive me. However, I had only known my grandfather for four or five days, and knew deep down that I had let him down by taking advantage of his hospitality in this way. No excuses. I should never have opened the trunk, I should have gone to him first and asked permission. That's what upset me most, not thinking it through enough. It was a horrible feeling letting down someone that I loved and who had been so kind to me, by snooping around and going through his things.

I stood in the kitchen, next to the huge table, nervously awaiting my fate. Grandpa eventually walked in and quietly said 'Follow me Danilo,' as he walked passed me, out into the garden and down to the logs right at the very end by the river, where we'd had our first chat just a couple of days earlier.

We sat in the sun in silence for a couple of moments before he spoke. I could sense that he was choosing his words carefully.

'Danilo. It is not a good thing to go looking through the property of other people without them knowing.'

'I know Grandpa, but I was only...'

Again, one wave of his hand silenced me immediately.

'Whatever reason you had, it was wrong. Do you know that?'

'Yes.' I nodded solemnly. 'I do.'

'Good. Now there is something Danilo that you must know. Everything I have here is for you,' as he motioned his hand in an arc that included the house, fields and outbuildings that were around us, 'but that does not mean that you can just look inside things without asking first. Do you understand?'

This time I just nodded. I could feel the tears coming and didn't want to risk saying anything in case I began to blub. I could sense him looking at me, but I couldn't look back at him.

'Ok,' he said loudly, clapping his hands onto his lap. 'Now we are clear on this, we will forget it and never mention this again. Shall we make a deal on that?'

Again I nodded, and a tear escaped from my eye and fell onto my cheek.

'Let's shake on it then,' my grandfather said and spat onto the palm of his open hand.

I put out my hand to shake his.

'You must spit too, Danilo,' he laughed, which I did, succeeding only in showering my hand with a mixture of spit and snot which the tears had loosened from my nose. My grandfather laughed out loud as he grasped my mucky hand. 'That is a very strong promise, stuck with all that snot!' and with that he gave me the tightest, most loving hug I think I'd ever had.

'Sorry, Grandpa,' I said, as I began to cry in his arms.

'Forget it now boy,' he said. 'It is finished. If the truth be known, I would have done the same as you in the same position, but I would have expected the same dressing-down too,' he smiled.

After a brief pause where I stopped crying and pulled myself together, he said: 'Right, after what you have seen in that box, I'm guessing you probably have some questions to ask of me – am I right?'

'Yes,' I smiled.

'Ok. Then, how is it you say – fire away?'

There was so much I wanted to ask that my brain was a bit scrambled, but then, all of a sudden after a moment's thought, came the most obvious question of all.

'Grandpa. Who is Fausto Coppi?'

My grandfather let out a big heavy sigh, closed his eyes, raised his head to the heavens and made a sign of the cross followed by what seemed to be a prayer in Italian.

'My son, your question is sadly wrong, but I wish with all my heart that it was correct. You see, you asked 'Who is Fausto Coppi?' Sadly, the correct question is 'Who was Fausto Coppi.' Again, my grandfather closed his eyes and sat in silence, shaking his head gently in regret. When he opened his eyes, they were moist, but he just wiped them with his shirtsleeve and began.

'Fausto Coppi was the finest man I ever knew. My own father I loved with all my heart, a brave, brave man who gave his life for the safety of me and his family. For years after his death at the hands of those terrible Germans, I never believed life was fair. I never believed I could live a truly happy life again. But then my path crossed with that of an exceptionally handsome young man, seven years older than me, who gave me back my life and taught me that life could again, be beautiful, that life could be wonderful. That man was to become my hero, and his name was Fausto Coppi.'

Again there was silence as my grandfather seemed lost in his thoughts.

'Do you have a best friend Danilo?' he asked finally.

'Yes I do, his name is Jamie,' I responded.

'Well, Fausto Coppi was my best friend. He was also my teacher and he was my guide. There was nothing that I wouldn't do for him. Nothing. And for him too, there was nothing he wouldn't do for me – or any of us. He was loyal and generous, two of the best attributes a friend could ever have.'

'I had no idea that he was your friend, Grandpa,' I said after a moment. 'I saw the pictures and the newspaper headlines, but I couldn't understand them because they were all in Italian. He looked like he was a good cyclist though.

My grandfather laughed at my comment. 'Oh yes, Danilo, you could say he was a good cyclist. He lived near here, he was from Castellania, no more than ten miles away. But, before I go on and tell you more, I must ask one promise from you. What I now tell you about Coppi – and in time, I will tell you everything – must once again remain between me and you. You must not tell your father, Danilo. He hates the name Fausto Coppi, so please do not speak to him of our conversations.'

I just nodded, already knowing that what my grandfather said was true having witnessed my father's reaction to Coppi's name when I asked him about him when we were sitting outside the coffee shop the day before.

'Ok,' my grandfather said, settling down and relaxing back on the log seat. 'Let's begin, but first, a question for you. I could tell from the way that you stood looking at that bike under the tarpaulin in the barn the other day, and the way you were entranced by the jersey Italia that you were holding earlier that you truly and deeply like cycling. Is this true?'

'Yes it is, Grandpa,' I replied straight back. 'I love all sports, but cycling is my absolute favourite. I watch the Tour de France every year on the TV.

'Ah, *La Grand Boucle*!' he shouted enthusiastically, 'Yes, a fine race, that is for certain. You say you watch the Tour now – do you have a favourite rider?'

'Yes,' I said instantly. 'Two, actually. My all-time favourite is Big Mig, but he's retired now,'

'Ah, Indurain,' my grandfather interrupted. 'Yes, he was quite good, there is no argument to that – who else do you admire?'

'Jan Ullrich,' I replied proudly.

'Ah yes, Ullrich. I have seen him. He has troubles in the mind though. This I see clearly with him. I already know that you could be better than him Danilo, this is obvious to me.'

I laughed: 'I will never be as good as those two Grandpa, they are brilliant.'

'Danilo, the first lesson to learn if you are to achieve your dreams is to believe. If you believe you can achieve something, you might. If you don't believe, you never will. A man without belief, is a man without life, this is simple. The first step is by promising to yourself that you will try to be the best that you can be. If you can achieve that, you may rest easy at the end of your life. Being the best you can be is the most important lesson you will ever understand in your life ... but I am getting ahead of myself, we will speak of that again.'

He paused. 'Now where were we? Ah yes, Coppi – was he a

good cyclist you asked? Let's see. How many Tours de France did your Big Mig win?'

'Easy,' I shouted. 'Five in a row'

I had read all about that. Big Mig was the fourth cyclist in history to win the Tour five times. I couldn't remember back then the names of the ones that did it before him, apart from knowing that one was called Merckx but I did know that the other two were Frenchmen. But, Big Mig was the only one to win five in a row. I must admit I was very pleased with myself and the raised eyebrows of my grandfather as I told him the answer, showed he was quite impressed.

'Very good Danilo, very good, you obviously know your stuff,' he smiled. 'Two Frenchmen called Jacques Anquetil and Bernard Hinault along with the Belgian Eddie Merckx are the only others to do it. Merckx was the best of that particular bunch by a very, very long way. But it is only fair and true that I say that Indurain was very good. But, another question, do you know how many of the major and important professional races Indurain won in his career, apart from the Tour de France?'

This time I was silent, I didn't have a clue.

'No? No matter, it is a very hard question, because we can talk about stage wins and overall wins. But, if we talk about overall wins, I know that Indurain won twenty-six other races. But what about my friend Coppi? Well, he did a little better Danilo, you see he won fifty-one of the important races – nearly twice as many as your Big Mig. Not bad no?'

'Wow,' I said. 'Fifty-one? Did he ever take part in the Tour de France?'

'Yes he did,' answered my grandfather triumphantly 'He was the first man after World War II to win it twice. I tell you, if it hadn't been for that hateful war that cost my father and so many other good people their lives, not to mention the many illnesses Fausto suffered because of the way he had to live in those terrible times, he would have won ten Tours de France, I have no doubt of that! But even without the opportunity to ride the Tour in those war years, he still managed to become the World Champion and also held the World Hour Record which only can be held by the fastest man alive. So, you say to me that Fausto looked like a good cyclist. I hope you can see now that, actually, he was a great one.'

I sat there for a moment looking at the pride that was just bursting from the face of my grandfather and tried to take in everything that he had told me about Coppi and his achievements. I had read quite a lot about Big Mig with Jamie, we used to test each other by asking ourselves questions about him after we found a book about him and his career in our school library. We were always in awe when we looked at the many pictures of him getting the prize after winning race after race. To think that Coppi had won so many more races than those of Mig that we'd read about in that book was absolutely incredible to me. But in all that I'd read about Big Mig, I never once remember reading about Coppi when they compared Big Mig's achievements to any other cyclists.

The name they did use though was Merckx, and the one thing I remembered about him was that they always said that he was the best of the 'modern cyclists.'

'Was Coppi not classed as being from the modern era then, Grandpa?' I asked.

'Excellent question!' my grandfather replied, smiling. 'No, he was not. The modern era really began with Merckx – The Cannibal. I'm sorry Danilo, but if Big Mig had raced at the same time as Merckx, your man would never have won a race, not one. Merckx was a genius on a bike. He did not pick and choose his races like many today, he raced in everything. He was an animal on the bike, he would attack and attack until he just demoralised his opponents, who became very happy to just fight for second place. But do you know, when Merckx dominated so completely as he did in the 60s and 70s, the people who write about the history of cycling, who write about who came before, only compared him to one man ... Fausto Coppi. Merckx, they said, was the Coppi of the modern era, and Coppi was the champion of the classic era. You see Danilo, the classic era took place straight after the war when we had nothing. The bikes weren't always of the best quality, the food certainly wasn't, if you were lucky enough to get any that is, and worst of everything were the terrible roads. The modern era had much more technology to thank for its advancements. Merckx, and all the riders that came along at the same time as him in the 1960s and 70s, had better bikes, better food, better training and, best of all, smooth tarmac roads. Fausto Coppi hardly had any of those great advantages. Professional cycling has always been hard, but in the classic era, quite simply my boy, it was brutal. It was a time that many experts believe to have been the hardest time ever to have been a professional cyclist and to have to race for a living. And it was then, in the toughest of times, that Coppi was king ... *Il Campionissimo.*

'That's the word,' I exclaimed excitedly. 'That's the word you said the other day and the one I saw in a headline on one of the pink papers ... *Il Campionissimo.*' I repeated it slowly, slightly mucking it up.

My grandfather paused as he began to speak, getting lost in his thoughts again.

'Yes, *Il Campionissimo, Il Campionissimo,*' he repeated softly. 'Do you know Danilo, there have been many, many Champions in cycling. Anquetil, Merckx, Hinault, even your Indurain and so many others, and now this American Armstrong, who I do not trust. Most of these were good men and all were Champion cyclists, no doubt about that. But only one cyclist in history has ever been called *Il Campionissimo*, only one, and that was Coppi.

He paused again.

Then, looking at me with a fire of pride burning deep within his dark eyes, he said: 'It means Champion of Champions, Danilo.'

'Champion of Champions.'

16

BEFORE I'd had any more opportunity to learn more from my grandfather about this apparently wonderful man and cyclist, all Fausto Coppi stories were put on hold due to a lorry arriving at the farm, beeping noisily as it entered the farmyard.

'Sewerage Company,' my grandfather explained, getting up from the logs.

'Sewerage Company?' I asked.

'Yes,' he replied with a smile, and then laughing said, 'the shit man Danilo ... now there's a good job for you, enough of these silly dreams of cycling!' and off he went, laughing out loud.

He was such fun my grandfather, yet amongst all his funny sayings and jokes, he often said something that went straight to the centre of my brain, something really key and important.

'Be the best that you can be.'

He'd kept on about that all morning. I didn't really get it at first until he explained it further. His main point was that most people have a talent for something in life, whether that's cycling, football, running or any skill you can think off. He even said that his principle was also the same for someone who wanted to be a farmer, a builder or a painter. He explained it to me by comparing two cyclists. He told me to imagine that one was naturally talented with a real gift to do well at it, but the other wasn't half as good. Then he said that the gifted one hardly ever trained or practiced, but the less talented one trained and practised and worked hard all the time to make himself almost as good as the more talented one.

My grandfather then asked me which one I thought was the better cyclist. I replied quickly that it was obviously the talented one. My grandfather shook his head gently and said it wasn't, and wouldn't ever be, but that most people make the same mistake. The talented cyclist in this case, he explained, will always regret not practising harder. Even if he wins a race, he will know deep down in his heart that he could have won the race better, by a bigger margin, crushing the opposition. Then, when he eventually comes up against cyclists of equal talent, but with the commitment of the less talented cyclist, he will find that he will only come in second or third at best. This means he will always wonder if he could have won these races, if only he'd trained and prepared harder. He will always wonder if he could have done more. Ultimately, he will always carry regrets in his heart he said. 'Regret is the curse of the person who doesn't give 100 per cent' he said. But moving on to the less talented cyclist, my grandfather explained that because he had trained to his absolute maximum and had given everything he could possibly give in a race, even though he may well be disappointed if he only finishes 10th or 11th, he will know in his heart, when he walks away, that he had done everything he could in his power to win. He could look himself in the mirror and see that he had delivered on his promise to 'be the best that you can be.' Any disappointments he may have about where he eventually ended up in a race will, in time, be softened by the fact that he could have done no more, he had nothing left to give. My grandfather said that a cyclist with that commitment will always be able to sleep well at night. As for the other cyclist, my grandfather said that he will probably be lying awake wondering 'Could I have done more?'

My grandfather said that he'd met so many men in his life who were much more talented than he was, but many of them now looked back on their life with huge regrets that they hadn't tried harder, and made the most of their talent, whether it be in farming or anything else. They felt they had wasted their talents and it haunted them. But he explained that even though he never felt he was particularly talented, he made sure that nobody tried or practiced harder than him at whatever the task was. He said that if even that meant that he still wasn't good enough, that was fine. At least he had tried to be the best that he could be. There will never be any shame in losing if a man can honestly say that.

I was beginning to understand.

Not long after the man with the smelliest job in the world had left with the farm's sewage, my dad returned with my grandmother from their trip into town. The amount of food she brought out from the boot was more than my mother would buy in a month. As she shuttled back and forth from the car to the kitchen, she started speaking to me excitedly and my father, laughing, told me to expect a very large lunch.

I don't think I had ever eaten so much food at one sitting. It was absolutely ridiculous, but also unbelievably delicious. Halfway through, when I was having about my fifth meatball, my father noticed with a wry smile that I'd seemed to have made a remarkable recovery from my 'illness' of the morning.

'Well, I did miss out on breakfast,' was the best excuse I could come up with to explain my gluttony.

He laughed and said: 'Well, I'm very pleased that your appetite has returned Dan.'

I carried on eating, because, well, so did everyone else, and after about an hour at the table, I honestly thought I was going to burst.

'Dad, tell Grandma that I wish she had a bed underneath the table, I'd just get straight under there and go to sleep.' My father translated, resulting in a huge burst of laughter and a sloppy kiss from my gran. Then she got the machine gun out again and rattled off a few quick-fire sentences to my dad who nodded in agreement.

'Mamma says that after a meal like that you should really have a traditional Italian afternoon.'

'What's that?' I asked

'A good kip!' my father laughed. 'Go ahead' he said to me 'go up and have a lie down on the bed for a couple of hours, you're allowed to – you're on holiday.'

I must admit, after all the food I'd eaten, it seemed like a great idea, so up to bed I went.

I was obviously a bit more tired than I thought.

'Come on Danilo, wake up, wake up!'

For a moment I thought I was being woken by Fausto Coppi, I'd had so many dreams about him, it would have made perfect sense, but instead it was my dad. Why was he waking me, I'd only been asleep about half an hour.

I gave out a massive yawn, rolled over and looked at my dad who was smiling, with the sunlight streaming through the window behind him.

'That was some sleep son,' he said, 'you've slept for nearly twenty hours!' he exclaimed. 'I was starting to get a bit worried about you.'

'Twenty hours?' I asked with surprise, sitting up. I thought he was joking. 'You mean it's tomorrow morning already?' I said as I stretched and yawned again. 'Has Grandma done breakfast yet?' I asked.

'Oh, I can see you are back to normal,' he laughed. 'Yes, it's all laid out on the table. Listen, Danilo. You remember when we went to town I mentioned my friend Franco?'

I nodded as I still tried to shake my mega-kip out of my bones.

'Well, he called around last night when you were sleeping and asked me to go out with him for the day. I said I'd wait until I spoke to you before letting him know because I'm aware that I haven't spent that much time with you since we've been here, so I just wanted to check it's ok with you first.'

'It's fine Dad, no probs,' I said with a smile. I no longer disliked my dad as much as I had when we arrived here, and that was mainly because every chance that he had, my grandfather would tell me what a good man he was. I actually wouldn't have minded going off with him and Franco and spending the day with them, but I also knew that with Dad away for the day again, it meant I could have another day with Grandpa. And that meant more stories about Fausto Coppi and the contents of that trunk.

'What time will you be back?' I asked.

'No later than six. You are sure this is ok?'

'Of course, no probs, see you later.'

And that was that. Dad was gone again, I pigged out on another huge breakfast and then went in search of my grandfather. When I saw him, I knew it was good news.

He was dressed in beige again.

17

*

I WAS standing outside the barn, leaning on my fantastic bike and adjusting the pair of sunglasses my grandfather had just given me. They were very old, but I must admit I thought they looked kind of cool in a retro way. Then the man in beige emerged from the barn, pushing his old black bike out into the sunshine again.

'Danilo, the best way to learn about *Il Campionissimo* is out there,' he pointed toward the network of lanes behind the farm, 'out on the roads.'

I didn't need any more convincing.

We set off and in no time we were alone on the deserted roads, with Grandpa giving me some practical tips about my posture on the bike. He said I needed to get a little lower on the bike, which meant I'd be leaning slightly further forward, but that essentially, it was all about comfort. It really felt better being slightly lower, it didn't seem as though I had to make so much effort to pick up speed and my legs seemed to be a little more relaxed as they spun round.

Soon we were cruising through the empty roads, and after a few miles we resumed our conversation about Coppi.

'So, Fausto Coppi was the best cyclist you ever saw then Grandpa?'

'Without a shadow of doubt yes,' he shot back. 'Some say his great rival Gino Bartali was his equal, but I only saw him when he was older, and whilst they would often be more interested in beating each other rather than winning the race they were in, when Coppi was free from injury and illness, Bartali couldn't touch him. Of course Merckx was amazing, a true force on the road, but as I told you before, he benefited from a lot of good things when money really went into cycling. So for me, Coppi was the King.'

I still found it amazing that from what my grandfather was saying, Coppi was one of the best cyclists of all time, but I still didn't know how he came to give my grandfather all his kit that was kept in a dusty old trunk, in the bathroom cupboard. I needed to find out.

'How did you end up with all his jersey's and kit then Grandpa?

'Pardon me boy – I don't understand,' replied my grandfather looking genuinely confused.

'Coppi's kit,' I repeated. 'The jerseys and shorts in the trunk with all the newspapers and scrapbooks about him. All his stuff you caught me looking at the other day, you know, and that fantastic Italian jersey'

My grandfather started to laugh until he saw the confusion etched all over my face. 'I'm sorry, I haven't explained myself fully have I boy?' he said. 'This stupid old man is getting very forgetful in his old age. I thought you knew, but how would you have known, I'd forgotten to tell you and of course there's no way that your father would have told you.'

'Told me what?' I asked, even more bewildered.

'Ok, Danilo. Those jerseys, those shorts and all that kit never belonged to Fausto Coppi, I can tell you that for sure.' he said seriously.

With that bombshell from my grandfather, I was, for about the tenth time on the trip, gutted. Even after the relatively small amount of information that he'd given me about Coppi, I could see that he was an extremely special cyclist – one of the best ever – and I was beginning to adopt him as my new hero. I was actually looking forward to getting home and going to the library to try and find out if any books had been written about him, so I could learn even more about his career. And if I was being totally honest, I was also hoping that by the time I made it back to the library at home, I'd have been wearing one of those Coppi jersey's on my back, no matter how big it was, perhaps as a gift from my grandfather for showing an interest. But now, there I was, being told by my grandfather, that the jerseys didn't even belong to Coppi. I was so disappointed.

'What about the Italian jersey?' I asked quietly. 'Didn't that belong to Coppi either?'

'No, it didn't. Like I say, none of that stuff did.'

I was gutted. I thought about all the newspapers and the scrapbooks that featured Coppi. Why would all those books and newspapers be kept in there if none of the kit belonged to him? I didn't understand. 'Who do all the newspapers and scrapbooks belong to then?' I asked.

'Well that's easy, Danilo, me. I kept everything that was ever written about Fausto Coppi from the day I met him. He was my friend, but he was also my hero, that is a very nice situation to find yourself in. Whenever I read about one of his many victories or perhaps of his heroic performances in the mountains, where he had no peer, I made sure that the first thing the next day, I would buy the newspaper and keep it. If it was a small piece, then I'd cut it out and would stick in the scrapbooks. I have twelve scrapbooks in total. My plan, at the end of his career, was to present it all to him in grateful thanks for all he had done for cycling in Italy. But sadly, the Lord above saw to it that my plan would be spoiled. That is why I keep them now as a shrine to him – private to me – in that trunk. That's why I was so annoyed when I saw you looking through it'

I apologised again, but then was quiet for a second as I tried to hide the disappointment of finding out that none of the stuff in the trunk belonged to Coppi. After a couple of minutes though, I realised that there was still a question I needed to ask.

'Well if they aren't Coppi's jerseys, whose are they then?'

For the first time since I'd met my grandfather, he looked a little timid and humble. After looking down at the road in front of us for a moment, he looked back at me, and said very quietly, almost by way of apology,

'Mine Danilo ... all the jerseys are mine.'

I nearly choked.

'What?!' I screamed excitedly. 'Yours? The jerseys are yours? Really? But wait a minute! You mean you were a cyclist, Grandpa?'

I was so thrilled and excited that the bike wobbled beneath me as I lost concentration. 'But you told me that you were a farmer. You said that after your father died in the war you and your brother looked after the farm!'

By now, the sheer excitement of this stunning revelation had made me lose my total focus in riding the bike, so I braked, stopped, got off and walked it over to the edge of the ditch to take in this unexpected bombshell. I lay the bike against the side of the ditch, then I started to walk up the shallow bank and sat down, facing the strong mid-morning sun, shaking my head in disbelief while looking at my grandfather for answers, who was also now slowly dismounting.

'Ok, Danilo, let me explain. I was a farmer,' he said, as he lay down his bike and joined me on the bank. 'I always have been a farmer and still am, I have told you no lies about that. But you remember I told you that when I first met Fausto he showed me how life could be beautiful again?' I nodded eagerly. 'Well that was when we nearly crashed into each other out on these very roads. I was shooting around on my bike, so full of the anger and hatred for the Germans who had killed my father that I hardly looked to see who was on the road around me. I had no care for my safety. But one day, Fausto came around a bend, going faster than me of course, and luckily, he saw me for I didn't see him. He swore at me because I nearly hit him, so I stopped and got off my bike to fight him, so angry did the fire burn within me in those days. But one look at his smile, as broad as a rainbow, from that tanned, slim, handsome face, meant that all the anger left me instantly. I had no money for water bottles in those days, but Fausto could see that my mouth was gummed up with thirst, so he insisted I finished the contents of his. We then just sat and talked for what seemed like ages, just as two young people getting to know each other always do. But, the thing that embarrasses me to my core to this very day, is that I had no idea who he was! Even though by then not only had he been a professional cyclist for many years, but he had already won the Giro d'Italia, Italy's own Grand Tour! The trouble was, because we were so poor we obviously had no television or never even bought newspapers back then so the only time I had heard the name Coppi was on the radio. I had no idea what he looked like, so I just thought this man was a simple farmer's son like me.' I sat transfixed, listening to my grandfather's unbelievable story unfold, open mouthed.

'Anyway, as we both got up to go, he asked me how far away from Castellania I lived. When I told him, he said that anyone that could cycle as fast as I had done, with my head down not looking where he was going, had the making of a great cyclist.'

My grandfather laughed out loud before continuing.

'There and then he asked if I'd like to meet him the next day for a training ride. I told him I couldn't because of my farming commitments, but he said he'd come at six o'clock in the morning if he had to. I chuckled and told him I would have been up milking for an hour by then. He burst out laughing and we subsequently agreed that we'd meet after evening milking. I didn't really think that this stranger would turn up, but then, at the appointed time at the same spot, there he was waiting. Do you know what Danilo?' my grandfather asked without waiting for my answer, 'it wasn't until three weeks later and after about ten training rides that he told me who he was. And that was only because he had a cycling training top I'd never seen him wear before that had BIANCHI on it. When I saw it, I was immediately envious, me in my worn out old working shirt, so I joked with him and said 'Who do you think you are ... Fausto Coppi?'

He just laughed and said: 'Yes, I am Umberto my good friend. Yes, I am.'

When Coppi said that, I sat on my bike, frozen with shock ... me cycling with the great Fausto Coppi, a name I'd only ever heard on the radio! I was embarrassed that I had not known who this great man was, but Fausto would have none of it, he was so humble. He told me: 'Umberto, it has been a long time since anybody treated me as I want to be treated, just as a young cyclist from Castellania. That's why I gave you my first name, Angelo, when we met, not Fausto, my middle name and the one my family chose to use.'

As I sat there, listening to my grandfather's story unfold, I just shook my head in disbelief and wonder at the story he was laying out before me. After a moment of silence, I urged him to continue.

'You see, Danilo, Fausto was surrounded with people all his life who he couldn't always trust. People who wanted that bit extra from him because he was able to attract the riches and the money, and these ruthless people only wanted to know him for those reasons. If you walk close enough to the apple cart Danilo, plenty of apples will fall out to prevent you ever getting hungry.'

I smiled in agreement at the remark, but had no idea what he was talking about.

He continued: 'I think what he liked about me from the start was that I had shown how ignorant I was by not knowing who he was, so I think he knew that a dumb farmer like me was someone he could trust and rely on. He was absolutely correct about that.' My grandfather said with great sincerity and pride in his voice. 'I can look you in the eye my lovely grandson, and tell you that I never denied Fausto Coppi, not once in his life. There are many who like to say that and pretend that they were loyal to him until the end, but not many of those people really believe it to be true when they look at themselves in the mirror. They know they let him down. I was loyal to him for all the years I cycled with him as his team mate, through thick and thin, right to the very end. It is my life's proudest achievement.'

Again my grandfather paused, and looked to the heavens. I too looked to the heavens, but for a different reason. I was trying to take in what he had just told me. Here was a man I'd only met that week, yet was one of the closest relatives I would ever have in my life. I had just thought that he was a humble Italian farmer, maybe a little crazy, and someone who despite his many wise sayings, probably didn't know much about life and the big wide world. But now I was coming to terms with the news that the truth was much, much different. This lovely, loyal, principled old man now appeared to have lived the life that I so longed to live ... the life of a professional sportsman, and not just that, a professional cyclist too.

'Be the best that you can be?' It was all starting to make sense to me now. That must have been exactly what he did. He went from being a farmer to a professional cyclist with Fausto Coppi. He absolutely must have been the best he could be.

I sat there amazed. But I had to know more.

'So how long were you a professional cyclist for then, Grandpa?' I asked eagerly.

'For 13 seasons,' he replied instantly, '1946 to 1959 – the best years of my life.'

'And were you a teammate of Coppi's all that time?'

'Every day, Danilo. From the day we met on these roads until injuries to my knees after a bad crash in the Milan – San Remo, my last race, forced me to stop in '59, I was at his side. Every day. I would have done anything he asked of me, without the slightest hesitation or the slightest thought. I trusted him more than any other man I have ever known, and it is my dearest hope Danilo, that he thought that of me too.'

'But I still don't understand, Grandpa. You said that you've been a farmer all your life with your brother, so how could you have been a cyclist too?'

'That is true, and as I have told you, I was – and still am a farmer. You see, I was truly blessed. Not only did I have a wonderful friend in Fausto, I also had a wonderful brother in Claudio. In those days, the season of cycling was much shorter than it is now. It ran very much from late spring to late summer – March to September – so that meant the unimportant cyclists like me had to find jobs in the winter. An important cyclist like Fausto had all year round contracts and advertising work to see him through the quiet months, but for the rest of us, we had to find work when the season was ended. Most in my position managed to find work in bicycle shops, or some even owned their own shops and built their own bikes for sale from any winnings they had made in the summer. Me? I put all the money I had earned and won back into the farm for the rest of my family to have. That was the deal I made with Claudio. He allowed me to go off for the summer to live out my dream riding at the side of *Il Campionissimo* and in return, I gave all my money to the farm and worked it with Claudio for the six months between autumn and spring. It was a deal made in heaven and I was happy to do it. Those thirteen years were the finest ever and they taught me that honest hard work and the earning of a fair day's pay was the most important thing a man can do in his life. And Danilo, let me tell you, I loved my life.'

Trying to take in the news I had learnt from my grandfather, I got up from my seat on the bank, reached forward for the water bottle on my bike, took a swig, then turned to face him again, pointing to my bike resting in the ditch.

'So, this bike, Grandpa, the one I ride and the name that has been scratched off – was that your name next to the Italian flag?' I asked. 'To match your Italian jersey?'

My grandfather's face changed instantly, with a deep sigh accompanying the frown that suddenly stretched across his face.

'No that is another story,' he said, 'a very sad story I'm afraid. In time I will get to that, I promise. But first we must get back on these bikes and continue our ride before these old bones of mine start to get too stiff.'

18

*

WHEN we re-mounted our bikes and set off over the country lanes along the plains that ran for miles up to the base of the Apennine Mountains which, apparently, stretched the whole length of Italy, I sensed that my grandfather wanted some silence. Whenever he talked about Coppi, it followed the same pattern. First he would be full of enthusiasm about him, telling story after story at the rate of a machine gun, before suddenly becoming quiet and sad, as though something was upsetting him deep down inside. When I recognised this, I would be quiet for a while or just talk about something not so obviously related to Coppi. But it was very hard, because I wanted to know everything about him, and just as importantly, wanted to know everything possible about my grandfather's career as a professional cyclist. I was still finding it difficult to take that very fact in. We cycled on for a while in silence when I noticed for the first time how high the mountains began to climb, and how steep they started to look, the closer we got to them. I pointed toward them, turned to my grandfather and asked: 'Have you ever cycled up mountains as high as that?'

His laugh was the only reply I needed. 'Yes my boy, many times and also many times up mountains much higher and steeper than those. And usually, when I started to climb them, it wouldn't be long before Fausto would leave us all behind and then we'd have to climb them on our own. But that was all in the future after that first time I'd bumped into Fausto and begun to ride regularly with him, because that happened in the spring of 1946, the year after the war finished. I had so much work to do on the farm at that time, we were just coming out of the war it is true, but still everything was scarce. You had to beg, steal or borrow equipment just so we would be able to plant, tend and harvest the fields. You see, the war had left Italy totally ruined and there was nothing like any luxuries, even good, healthy food was scarce – as it had been throughout the war years – and it was this lack of nutrition that, in time, would cost Fausto a lot of pain.'

'Pain? Why was that?' I asked.

'Well, unknown to us in the early days, Fausto had been a very sickly child. There had been so little food about in those days leading up to, and during the war, especially the food that was needed to give you the nourishment that all young children require in order that they will develop into strong adults. As a sportsman, Fausto would have needed even more than a normal person would have required, but his body had been denied of this in his crucial, early development years. By the time that I got to know him, the result was, that on the outside, Fausto's body gave the impression that he was the fittest man in the race, but on the inside, his body was the worst of us all. His bones were weak and extremely brittle which is a huge problem for a cyclist. You see, an occupational hazard for a professional cyclist is a crash. A day hardly passed by, in both training and competition, where one of us didn't crash. To us, a normal crash simply left us battered and bruised with some grazing that we called 'road rash', no real problem, just something to be tolerated. But to Fausto, a similar straightforward accident often resulted in the curse of the cyclist – broken bones. I lost count of the number of breaks he endured, it was incredible. There were times in his career when he would be in the form of his life, so far ahead of his main competitors, that they had simply no chance of bettering him. Then, out of the blue, he would suffer a simple accident, and while we were hoping he would just get straight back up, down he would stay, only to be told by the doctors that he had suffered another break. It seemed that he was always having to battle back from one injury or another. Mind you, he was also brave, sometimes too brave, and if it was humanly possible, he would get back on his bike and complete the race. We had such respect for him for that – he would never, ever give in to pain. He remains the bravest cyclist I ever knew. But it was not just his bones,' he continued, 'his body was not very strong to fight the coughs and colds that we all carried within us at some time or other. Any virus that was going around, Fausto caught it and always his dose was the worst of us all. You know, when I think of what he achieved with such a weak body, it is truly incredible. The good Lord blessed me with the constitution of an elephant, and I tell you this with total certainty, if I could have given Fausto my body, well then I simply cannot see how he could ever have been beaten. He certainly paid the price for his malnutrition suffered in his childhood, but even on top of this neglected start to his life, he suffered further bad luck in his youth which didn't help him in later life in terms of the health you need to be a cyclist.'

I wondered if my grandfather was referring to a lack of food again, but two words put me right straight away.

'The War.'

'Why the war?' I asked. 'What happened to him?'

'He was taken prisoner.'

'Prisoner?' I asked excitedly. 'Like in a prisoner of war camp?'

'Exactly, Danilo. As I told you, Fausto was older than me – that was his bad luck – and that meant he had to fight. Do you know about Italy in the War boy?'

'Only a little bit that we've done in history in school,' I replied, 'I know that they were friends of Hitler.'

'Hah,' spat my grandfather loudly. 'They were,' he said pointing toward the hills, 'those fascist bastards in Milan.' This time he spat for real, with anger onto the road as we cycled, just flying past my front wheel as we went.

'I am sorry to swear and spit Danilo, but I am still very angry of that time. It was they – Mussolini ... *Il Duce*…as he liked to be called and his cronies.' The name Mussolini caused my grandfather to spit again, sadly without the accuracy of his previous one, his left foot catching the full impact of his flob, but he didn't seem to notice, and carried on without pause. 'He caused the death of my father, jumping into bed with Hitler. I for one cheered when they hung his and his mistress's body in the square in Milan. If I could have, I would have cycled there and spat on them both like so many of my countryman did. That pig. He even looked like a pig, and that is how he died ... like a pig.'

I was quite surprised at this rant by my grandfather, he was usually so happy and calm, so to witness such strong anger in him was a surprise. I think he noticed I was shocked and after a couple of minutes of cycling in silence, he spoke again.

'I apologise again for my anger. It is my sincere wish that you never have to witness a war, it does terrible things to a person, and delivers such hate into their heart. My hate used to consume me, but as I told you earlier, it was Fausto and cycling that released all that hate ... but now and again, when I think of what fate befell my father, sometimes the hate returns. I am sorry to show you that.'

'I don't mind.' I said. 'When we did World War II in school last year, we covered the bit when Hitler bombed Swansea and blew up the biggest shop in the town and the cinema too, so I don't like the Germans either.'

I spoke with such seriousness, that my grandfather burst out laughing again.

'Then that makes two of us,' he smiled. 'Now where was I before I started on my rant?' he asked.

'You said that Coppi was a prisoner of war.'

'Yes, yes he was. And that was where his second piece of bad luck began. At first, at the outbreak, the war was very good for him. He was getting fed better than he had been at home – still only army rations – but much better than he was used to. The army liked Fausto too because he had already won the Giro d'Italia in 1940, where he first humiliated the great Bartali, so despite me not knowing what Fausto looked like, the rest of Italy did, so they were more than happy to use Fausto in every possible way. That of course, meant that he was still allowed to cycle and take part in races, but now he was representing the army, not his professional team. Because the war was going well for the Fascists at that time, they were more than happy to let him keep cycling whenever there were races. It meant that they could reflect in his glory.' I swerved slightly when he said the word 'fascists' in case he started spitting again, but obviously his anger had passed now.

'Fausto was initially treated like a bit of a celebrity and enjoyed privileges that were denied other soldiers, the best of those was that he wasn't sent to the front line to fight – and that is a very good privilege to have!' My grandfather laughed out loud at this point, before continuing. 'Then, in 1942, he went to the Vigorelli velodrome in Milan, to try to break the World Hour Record that had stood for five years. He told me years later that he did not do it for this reason, to show he was the fastest, instead, he did it because it delayed further his posting to the front lines, because when the army learned of his attempt at the hour record, they were happy to let him train and prepare for it, which meant he was kept away from the fighting. They knew that success for Coppi would also be seen as success for them.'

I interrupted at this point. 'Didn't Chris Boardman break the hour record too?'

'Yes, he did,' Grandfather nodded. 'As did your good friend Big Mig!'

'Really?' I exclaimed. 'Wow, I never knew that.'

'Not bad for an ignorant farmer, eh boy?' my grandfather screeched.

'No, not bad,' I laughed. 'So did Coppi break the record?'

'Yes, he did. But it was very hard work. He explained it all to me one day many years later when we were in a training camp in Switzerland after we had learned that Jacques Anquetil had just broken Fausto's record. He told me that for that hour on the bike in that famous old velodrome in Milan, it was only his sheer willpower that kept him upright toward the end. He had not been able to prepare for it as well as he had hoped, for many of the reasons I have already told you that were all to do with the war. If you had ever seen Fausto ride Danilo, then there is one thing that you would remember – he was so perfectly smooth and constant. But he told me that his body went through such torture, that it was impossible to keep a steady pace throughout. His progress through the hour saw him reaching speeds that would have seen him break the record by three hundred metres, all the way back down to speeds that would have seen him end up two hundred metres short. It was only afterwards, after the statistics of his ride were released that all the top cyclists of the time thought that if one as good as Fausto could struggle so much, then they would never try.'

'What do you mean when you say he could break it by three hundred metres, was it not a race then?' I asked.

'Not in the normal sense of the word, no. The 'Hour' is simply a race between the rider and the clock. Let me explain. Look up the road ahead of us. If that road was a never ending straight line, then the way that 'The Hour Record' works is that the bell would sound, and I would just cycle as far down that road as I could in an hour. So, let's say that after one hour, when the bell goes again, I have cycled twenty-five miles, then that would mean for you to beat me, you would have to cycle the same road for twenty-five miles and one inch, in the same one hour period to beat me. The Hour isn't measured in time, it is measured in distance. The one who rides the furthest distance in the hour becomes the record holder. Do you see my boy?'

'Ah, yes, I do now. But you said he did it on a track?'

'That's right, on the Vigorelli velodrome track in Milan.'

'Well how far did he cycle in the hour then?' I asked.

'A little over twenty-eight-and-a-half miles,' came his reply.

'Wow!' I exclaimed, trying to make sense of such a fantastic achievement. 'That's almost as far as it is from Swansea to Cardiff, that's unbelievable!

'Yes it is. He broke the existing record by thirty-one metres, which was more than enough to put people off breaking it for some time.'

'But you did say that – what's his name again? – Anquetil broke it Grandpa, so it couldn't have lasted long.'

'Yes, but what I didn't tell you was that when Fausto and me had that conversation in Switzerland about Anquetil breaking his record, it was a few years after he'd set it.'

'What, four or five years or something?' I asked

'It was just a little bit longer than that Danilo. Fausto's world record mark stood for fourteen years.'

Coppi's record had lasted for as long as I had been alive.

'That's almost my lifetime,' I said in wonder.

'In terms of cycling, it is a lifetime,' my grandfather said with a smile.

'Anyway,' he continued after a brief pause, 'after the hour record, the war started to go downhill for Italy, and for Fausto too. Within a year he was sent with his unit to North Africa, where he was soon captured by the British. He remained a prisoner of war until 1945. But it was while he was in a prison camp in North Africa where he was dealt his next bit of bad luck, which was to lead to him developing the weakness which meant he was unable to fight off the many viruses the rest of us managed to do later in life – he caught malaria.'

'I've heard of that,' I said. 'It's quite serious isn't it?'

'Yes, my boy it is, it can kill you, but it is too early in Fausto's story to tell you about that. Anyway, he was shipped back from Africa once he had recovered from the malaria, to another prison camp in the very south of Italy in a place called Caserta. When the war finally came to an end, with those German scum finally destroyed to the complete joy of the Italian people, Fausto was released. The trouble for him then was that because he had no money and nowhere to stay down in the south, he decided that there was only one thing for it, he had to get home, as quick as he could, back to the north and his family. A kind English soldier who, before his injuries received in the war, had himself been a professional cyclist, had befriended Fausto in the camp and then managed to find him a bike. So now, there was no decision to be made, Fausto cycled back to his home in Castellania, all the way from Caserta over five hundred miles away. It was a typically brave solution to many of the dilemmas that Fausto faced in his life. When he arrived back home, the Italy he had left some years before was a very different place, beaten and depressed as it was. Fausto however, knew exactly what he had to do. As quickly as possible, he had to get back into the shape he needed to return to cycling at the highest professional level. And do you know what? He achieved that goal by riding around these very roads ... just a little bit quicker than me and you are today,' Grandpa said, smiling.

'Gosh, that's amazing,' I said in wonder.

'But,' as Grandpa continued, 'Fausto never forgot the debt that he owed to that English soldier that helped him. He kept in touch with him, and later would meet him in Milano after the soldier met and ended up marrying an Italian girl from there, eventually settling in the city. Months later, when Fasuto began putting together his team for the first full cycling season after the war, he contacted the Englishman, and offered him to become the trainer and masseur, a role he carried out for the team until the very end. His name was Eddie.'

'Ah!' I exclaimed. 'So, is that why you speak such good English then Grandpa? I'd been wondering why, especially because the rest of the family speak so little.'

'You are a very smart kid, Danilo. Yes it is. I cannot put a number on the many hours I spent on the treatment table with Eddie working on my tired legs, getting them in shape for the next day of pain and suffering. In all that time I insisted he spoke only to me in English because I always believed I would need it at some point in my life, so it was important that I took the opportunity to learn. I know I do not speak it perfectly well, and sometimes, I – how you say? – "Cock it up," but I now know that I was right to learn, because if it had not been for Eddie, I would not be able to speak to you now, my beautiful grandson, so freely. You see, indirectly, I even owe this honour to Fausto' ... he paused for a moment, and his words tailed off ... 'I have never thought of that before.'

We stayed out on the roads for about another hour and a half or so, and in that time, he told me a few more stories about his training rides with Coppi and how they got to know each other well. In between, he kept looking at how I sat on the bike, the gears I chose to use, the speed my legs went round, and kept giving me tips all the time. All throughout though, he was encouraging. Not once did he shout, nag or lose his temper when I didn't understand exactly what he asked. All the time it was thoughtful encouragement, just building my confidence, always reminding me, again and again, to 'be the best that you can be'. He was the perfect teacher, the perfect coach. As we were heading back with the farmhouse in sight, and boosted by all the positive lessons he had been giving to me, I just started to dream that this was not just what I wanted to be, but was maybe even something I could actually be....a professional cyclist, just like my grandfather had been. It was the first time that I really believed that it could happen. I also knew that it would be up to me to make it happen – nobody else. And there would be no room for quitting. So I quit quitting right there on the spot.

19

✳

WE'D made decent time on our way back, the wind that there was, was at our backs, which made it that little bit easier for us both. We got to within about two hundred yards from the driveway up to the farm, when Granddad made his usual request,

'Don't forget now, not a word of this to your father. Our secret.'

This time, instead of just nodding, I simply asked: 'Why?'

My grandfather looked straight back at me and said: 'It is not easy for me to answer all of your questions, Danilo.'

With that, we both flung our bikes right, swung into the drive and cycled up to the point where the gravel began. We both saw it at the same time. And we both froze.

Dad's car was parked in front of the small barn.

This time, and for the first time, I saw a new emotion on my grandfather's face. Fear.

'Come quick,' he said. 'If we can get into the barn we can hide the bikes and pretend we have been in the fields walking. Mama will not tell your father where we have been, she would be too worried about what the outcome may be.'

I found all this secrecy a bit odd. It was obvious that the two of them didn't get on, my dad hadn't had a single conversation with his father since we'd arrived out here nearly a week ago. I'd worked out that they'd obviously had a big argument at some point in the past, and it was clear that both of them were too stubborn to make the first move to become friends again. I couldn't understand it though. Despite everything, I now knew my father was a good man, and the way my grandfather spoke of him when we were out cycling proved that, and the sadness in his voice when he spoke of him proved to me that he still loved him. And as for my grandfather himself, well,

I'd never met such a loveable, caring, thoughtful man in my life. The way he chose to teach me about cycling proved that, he was so considerate in the way he put his point across, making sure he didn't offend.

I just couldn't work out what must have happened to result in them disliking each other so much. But, before I could give it any more thought, my grandfather called quietly to me, in a voice that showed genuine fear.

'Quick, Danilo, no time now to drag your feet. To the barn with the bike.'

I jumped off the bike and caught Grandpa up just as he was reaching the dark entrance of the barn. Then Dad stepped out from its shadows and into the sunlight.

I had never seen a person look so angry in my whole life, and he wore a look on his face that I had never seen on anyone before. He was silent for a moment, then exploded with rage.

'What the bloody hell do you think you are doing?' He screamed at my grandfather, his face as red as the Wales rugby jersey I was wearing, and the veins on the side of his head bulging like some maniac out of a horror film. I had never seen a human being look so infuriated. I was terrified.

'Please, Luca,' my grandfather replied softly and calmly, with his great hands held up in front of him. 'In Italian, not for the boy to hear,' glancing at me as he spoke.

'Not for the boy to hear? Not for the boy to hear?' my father roared, 'It's exactly for the boy to hear ... your new pupil deserves to know everything there is to know about his cycling coach, the former Bianchi professional cyclist, Umberto Rossi.' My father said mockingly, waving his arms about dismissively.

'Please, Luca, my boy,' he protested. 'It is between us, we need to sort this out once and for all, but please let the boy be with his grandmother, she will take him, he doesn't need to witness this.'

I looked to my right at the farmhouse and there, standing by the door, her hands clasped to the handkerchief that covered her mouth in horror, was Grandma, her eyes filled with fear. I lay my bike down on the gravel and moved to walk towards her.

'Stop! You stay right there Danilo,' my father barked at me. 'You will listen to all of this ... it is time you learned the truth about me, but more importantly, your grandfather.'

I stopped dead, rooted to the spot. I didn't know what to do. It was strange, because even though I think I should have been, I was no longer scared or emotional, or even concerned about what was going to take place. I think I was just confused more than anything, but part of me, if I'm really honest, was thrilled. I did want to know what had happened between these two key people in my life and I had never seen my father speak with such passion. I realised that what I was about to witness was going to make sense of lots of issues that had been rolling around in my mind for years. So there I stood, bizarrely almost looking forward to what they were about to say.

My father began walking slowly toward my grandfather, his feet crunching over the gravel as he walked, the only sound, breaking the eerie silence. I looked straight at my grandfather, he just stood there, head bowed slightly, as if in shame. Then, with his temper seemingly under a bit more control, my father started speaking to his father.

'My son there,' he said, pointing at me. 'Do you know that he has hated me? Despised me? Do you know that?'

Now it was my turn to hang my head in shame.

'And do you know why he has hated me?' he said coldly to his shocked father. 'Do you?'

My grandfather nodded slowly in response.

'That's right, of course you do. Because I hate cycling. Isn't that unbelievable? My own father is a former professional cyclist, my son would like nothing more than to become a professional cyclist, and he's hated me because he thinks I was useless at sport and that I hate cycling! A useless cyclist and a useless sportsman who was no good at any sports in school. That is the picture my son has had of me for as long as I can remember. That was the reason for my own son's hatred.'

My grandfather spun round to look at me, tears in his eyes.

'No Danilo, this is not true, not true at all. Your father was a beautiful sportsman, he loved his sport. Why do you think this of your father? Why do you think he was no good?'

As I blushed, embarrassed at the question, and before I could even begin to think of an answer my father spoke again. Loudly.

'Don't you dare ask him,' he barked, 'leave him out of it. He thinks that way because that's what I led him to believe. It was easier to have him believe that than have to tell him the sorry truth.'

He paused at this point, just glaring at his father, who said nothing, just stood there, knowing that he just had to take whatever it was that my father was about to throw at him. Dad continued: 'When his mother and me split up he was only four. From then on I only saw him on weekends. So, from beyond my reach he found comfort in the one thing I hated ... sport. And as he grew older, his love of sport developed into the one area of it that I hated more than anything else...cycling. I couldn't believe it,' laughed my father, 'here I was, wanting to bring my son up as a fit, proper and respectful person, and the only thing he wanted was cycling....the one thing I couldn't give him. And whose fault is that my father? Whose fault is it that I turned my back on the sport I once loved? On the cycling I once loved? So much so that I would rather let the boy I loved more than anything in my life believe I was useless at it. Huh? I didn't hear you? Whose fault was that? Tell me.'

After a long silence, my grandfather whispered: 'It was mine. It was all my fault Luca. I am so terribly, terribly sorry,' he said and began walking toward his son, with his heavy arms outstretched in front of him.

'You stay there,' shouted my father immediately. 'We haven't finished this yet'.

I was now so confused, I couldn't think properly. My dad was always rubbish at sport, he'd always told me that. He always hated cycling, he told me that too. It had always been that way for as long as I could remember. But hang on, that wasn't right. It all started to dawn on me. I had always told my father that he was no good at sport, because he'd never shown any interest in it, which frustrated me so much. I had always told my father that he must have been no good at cycling, because he had never encouraged me in it, which frustrated me further. And when I told him that, in my spoilt little way, he had never said anything in his defence which would have made his life a hell of a lot easier. Instead, he just allowed me to believe that. He had allowed me to believe that because he had decided that it was easier for him to let me hate him, than it was for him to tell me whatever the ugly truth between him and my grandfather was. I was quickly realising that I had sadly got my father all wrong these past few years. And that started to make me angry. Very angry.

'Hold on,' I shouted, breaking the temporary silence that had fallen on the argument.

'Dad. Are you saying you were good at sport when you were young? Good at cycling?'

My father said nothing, just looked away, embarrassed.

My grandfather spoke to me instead. 'Your father is a very proud man,' he said, 'and an extremely modest one too. He was the most talented sportsman in our family, the most talented cyclist in our family. It breaks my heart that you knew nothing of this until now and it breaks it further to know that it is I who am responsible for the wedge that was driven between you both. My fault, Danilo, totally my fault.' His words tapered off quietly as he shook his head in sorrow.

'Why is it your fault, Grandpa? What did you do?' I demanded. 'What did you do?'

Nothing. My grandfather just stood there. All I could hear were the sobs of my grandmother.

I was starting to turn red now, and then the anger really came. 'What did you do? What did you do to him?' I shouted, pointing at my father.

After a moment's thought my grandfather spoke. Almost silently.

'I broke him, Danilo. I broke him.'

The tears streamed now, but not down my face, but that of my grandfather. His dark, rugged face became stained as they fell in torrents. He wasn't sobbing or crying, these tears just poured and poured from him without any other sign of emotion.

'I broke him, Danilo,' he repeated.

I turned when I heard another noise, the sound of my father beginning to sob.

'What do you mean broke him?' I said, turning back to my grandfather. 'I don't know what that means.'

'Let me explain,' he sighed. 'By the age of 14, your father was the best cyclist in Alessandria. By 15, he was the best in Piedmont. And sadly, I became a very different man as a result. I was obsessed. Obsessed with cycling, obsessed with winning. I knew that my son was gifted, I knew that my son was going to be a professional, but I wanted more from him, still more. I wanted him to be the best there had ever been. I wanted him to be Coppi.'

'Be the best that you can be,' you told me.' I interrupted angrily, annoyed that it seemed that my grandfather was intending to take me down that same path as he'd taken his own son before destroying him. 'What you really mean is to become another Fausto Coppi?!'

'No, Danilo,' he responded instantly. Now it was his turn to get angry. 'That is not what I want for you at all. I believe in my heart that all you can ever ask of anyone is for them to be as good as they can possibly be, however good or bad that is. And that is all I genuinely want for you, nothing more than that. But, I can now say truthfully that I only learned this lesson after the heartbreak of losing my son, your father. I wanted him to be, not just the best, or even the best that he could be, I wanted him to be the best that there had ever been. Better even than Coppi. I would accept nothing less than that. Now I have learned that the dream of being the best has to be also the dream of the person themselves. I just didn't realise that at the time. My beautiful son Luca didn't want to be the best there had ever been. He just wanted to enjoy himself, have fun. If he won, he won, if he didn't, it didn't matter. I just couldn't understand that approach at the time. But please believe me Danilo, I do now. I now understand that winning really isn't everything, but I learned that too late. I lost my way Danilo, and I did some very bad things. I can admit that now.'

'Oh yes, you can admit that now,' said my father, his face now turned red and blotchy by the tears. 'Don't just think that this can end with you admitting that you did some bad things, and saying sorry. That's not enough. I have had 20 years of my life – and my relationship with my son – ruined, and he needs to know why. So let's tell my son some of the things you did when you still believed that winning was the only thing that mattered shall we?'

My grandfather groaned.

'Like the time you made me cycle home, alone, all the way from Stradella – 45 miles away – just because my foot came out of the pedal, do you remember that? As I tried to catch the leader who I'd mistakenly let make a break with ten miles to go?'

'At one point Danilo,' said my father looking at me, 'the leader was two minutes clear of me, a huge amount to make up in just ten miles. And by the finish, I'd got to within a single bike length of him when my foot slipped out because I was throwing so much effort in to pip him on the line. But because my foot popped out, it meant he beat me on the line. I had put so much effort into that final climb, pushing myself absolutely to the limit, that I had to be revived with oxygen at the finish and the people cheered my efforts when I'd recovered. But my father? Did he join the cheers? Did he come and check I was safe and well? No, he ignored me because he was so angry. He was so angry that I'd lost the race. He waited until I had recovered and then just told me that a good professional would never make such an error, would never have let the winner make a break like I had. A good professional would have won. He then made me cycle all the way home. Alone. It was nearly ten o'clock at night when I got in. But I wasn't supposed to be a good professional Danilo. I was just 15 years old'.

I turned and glared at my grandfather, horrified at what I had just heard, but he didn't see my glare, as his head was barely off his chest, so ashamed was he.

My father continued. 'Then we can add in the ridiculously hard training sessions. Every day – even Christmas day – I had to ride my bike. From the age of 11 until I was 17, every day I was made to ride my bike. Every day I was told I would never be as good as Coppi, that I wasn't fit to sit on the same bike that Coppi had. It got so that I hated the very mention of the name Coppi. My country's biggest ever Champion, the man who I used to love and dream of, I got to hate his very name. You taste the amount of cycling that my father made me swallow and I promise you Dan, you will learn to hate it too. And do you know what? The one thing that would have made it all right? The one thing that even through all my pain and exhaustion that still would have made it ok, the thing that I wanted more than anything? That just once, he would have said 'Well done. Well done my son.' But he never said it. Not once, not ever.'

I was stunned. This was so unlike the kindness and encouragement that my grandfather had shown me. Yet now, as I looked at this strong man, almost pathetic with tears running off his face and bouncing onto the gravel stones, I had a different view of him.

I hated him.

'Let me show you something.' said Dad, interrupting my thoughts, and off he disappeared into the barn. The barn where I'd first stumbled across the bike. My grandfather threw his head back and groaned, and made some sort of protest in Italian that I didn't understand. He obviously knew what was coming.

My father emerged carrying a big cardboard box, with a small rug over the top of it. He marched straight passed my grandfather as if he was invisible, and placed it at my feet.

'Danilo, if I had never seen you cycling with my father, I would never have asked you to do this. I knew that you had a right to have a relationship with your grandfather, but I simply could not allow that to stretch to cycling in case he tried to do to you what he had done to me. Please believe me my son when I tell you I am not a boastful man. I just ask you to do this to illustrate a point. Please, look in the box.'

I waited a moment, then crouched down, slowly removing the rug that covered the large box. I couldn't believe my eyes when they focused on the glittering riches that lay within. The first thing that stole my attention me were the colours, sparkling and glinting now that the contents were exposed to the light. Everything in there was either silver or gold. There were medals, trophies, cups and badges, along with frames, certificates and sashes. There must have been over fifty different awards in there.

I was stunned.

'These ... these were yours, Dad?' I asked in awe, looking up at my father with never before seen pride.

My dad nodded and said: 'And every time I won a new one, into the box it went and into the barn they stayed. 'Forget that, it's gone' he would say', pointing at my grandfather, 'just worry about the next one now.'

'And I'd never see any one of them again. This is the first time I have seen any single one of those since the day I won them.'

When I realised and understood just how many prizes were in the box, a monument to the excellence of my father, I just burst into tears. 'All that time I said you were rubbish,' I sobbed. 'All that time and you never said a word to me about these medals, these trophies.' I paused as the tears streaked down my face. 'I'm so ashamed ... I'm so sorry Dad,' I said, and flung myself into his arms.

'It is not your fault son,' he said hugging me tight. 'It is his.' He said pointing at his father, who was now sobbing openly. 'It is his.'

My dad pulled me closer, turned and began to walk me to his mother, also sobbing, at the back door. 'It is over now, my son, all over,' he whispered.

Then my grandfather said quietly through his tears: 'Wait. Please wait.'

But we carried on walking, ignoring him.

Then he shouted: 'WAIT, just WAIT!'

My father and I stopped, surprised at the desperation in my grandfather's voice, and slowly looked around.

'Danilo,' my grandfather began. 'Do you know how many medals are in that box? No? What about you Luca, do you?'

Both of us said nothing.

'Twenty-seven medals – twenty-four gold, three silver. There are also twelve cups – individual – and four more – team. There are sixteen certificates to commemorate the times you rode in age group races for Italy, and eleven gold sashes for your stage wins. Finally, there are nine individual trophies for your time trial victories.'

My father looked slightly taken aback.

'Every day, for the past twenty years since you have left Luca, I take one out, and look at it and remember what you did to achieve it, all your hard work and talent. I remember every breakaway, every hill climb and every time trial. Then, once every month – on a Sunday – I take everything out, lay them in order and clean them. It is the closest I ever get to being with you my son. I carry so much shame that I never once said, 'Well done' that if I could leave this earth now, and that meant I could have my time over to change it, and say well done – just once – all the years ago, I would. But it was different back then...'

Before he could say another word, my father started again.

'Oh, here we go – "It was different back then." You are just going to try to make Danilo see that you weren't that bad at all and just blame it on the fact that 'it was different back then'. Don't try to deceive my son that this only happened because times have changed.'

'Please, I am not going to do that Luca. I have too much respect for you to do that ... and you hadn't let me finish. Once I have finished what I have to say now, then you and Danilo can judge me, and I will then know if I have lost a grandson too, or hopefully re-gained a son.'

My father said nothing. Neither did I.

My grandfather paused then pointed at me. 'You remember you asked me whose name used to be on the bike next to the Italian flag?

Where the bare metal now sits?' My father's body visibly tightened as I nodded, remembering. 'It said 'Gianluca Fausto Rossi', your father. The day that bike was delivered by the manager of the Carrera professional cycling team, was the proudest day of my life. Prouder than anything I achieved in racing and prouder than anything I achieved at the side of Fausto Coppi.'

My father raised his eyes slightly at that last remark, as if recognising that it was a pretty big compliment for my grandfather to pay.

'But instead of telling the owner of the bike, my son, the one who with his own talent and hard work had earned that bike, how I felt, I said nothing. Standing here now, I cannot believe that a father could be so cold to his own son. Even if in my heart I was proud, I simply could not bring myself to say it. And there was only one true reason why that was. And I have told you this about me before Danilo. Ignorance. I was ignorant and I was stupid. You see, I never had someone to coach me, to tell me how to improve and get better. All I did was copy the best cyclist who ever lived – *Il Campionissimo* – for me that was a dream that became a reality, to have the opportunity of following Fausto Coppi so closely, but for my son, that very same name became a curse.'

He paused at this point as if searching for the right words.

'Once I realised that my Luca had talent, possibly more talent than even Fausto himself had possessed at a young age – and I still believe that to be true to this very day – I panicked. I was an ignorant farmer, who despite having earned my living in cycling, had never known how on earth to train somebody else to ride. People who knew I had been a cyclist and could now see the talent that your father had, would say: "Ah, Luca will be alright, he will have the perfect coach – his father." But in truth, I was terrified, I was so ignorant, I didn't know where to begin. So, as I mentioned, I panicked. I decided the only approach that I could offer was one of hard work, surely that would be the correct way I thought. I was used to that, and I was never shy of it. I worked like a dog to keep at Fausto's side when I raced. To him it all came so easily, so gracefully – exactly as it did to your father – but me? I had to work like a dog. So when I saw how easy it all was to your father, I made the terrible, terrible error of thinking that the only way for him to truly appreciate his talent and not to waste a single ounce of it was to work him hard for it. Work him as hard as I had to work for mine. Work him like a dog.'

His words tailed off into silence. My father just stared at him. I sensed, that for the first time ever, he was learning the sad truth behind his father's handling of him as a gifted young cyclist.

'Once I had started out on this hellish route, there was no way back. In fact, if anything, it became easier. It is always easy to be the bully. Nobody to challenge you, nobody to knock you down. The bully is a wonderful place to be. But do you know what being a bully does to you eventually my boy? It eats away at you from inside. First it makes you empty – the person you bully doesn't speak to you any more, doesn't look at you any more, finds ways to avoid you – then, the pain you know you are causing them starts to eat away at you, like a disease. Even when you then get challenged, as the brave Luca did to me when he turned sixteen, the bully doesn't care. He has now lost all compassion and carries within his heart only hate. And that is what I became, a bully filled with hate.'

Again he paused. I could see that every word he was saying was true, and was extremely painful for this proud man to deliver. But I knew that this man was no longer a bully, I had seen that with my own eyes, but it was clear that he had done terrible things to my father and maybe it was now right that he tortured himself this way. Maybe he needed to. Maybe my father needed to hear all this. Maybe we all did. My father and I remained silent as he continued.

'Then came the final day. The worst thing I had ever done to my son. The final humiliation. There is a steep hill climb not far from here. It takes about thirty-five minutes to climb, and sections are steeper than some of those that exist on Alpe d'Huez in the Tour de France. I had followed my son all the way to the foot of the climb in the wagon, and now took another road to the summit where he would finish, so that I could be there before him to watch him triumph. To my eternal damnation, all I could think of was Coppi. Luca looked so like him on the bike – as do you too – and I'd seen Coppi in this position a hundred times or more. As my son made his break at the bottom of the climb, I knew that Coppi would have won by a minimum of ten minutes in the same situation. I now expected my son to do the same. It was madness, he was only eighteen. We all waited the thirty-five minutes until the first rider came around the final bend. My son. I was elated. He powered to the line to rapturous cheers from everybody. Inside, my delight knew no bounds, but outside, I just stood, coldly with my hands rigid in my pockets. Ignorant, refusing to share my hidden joy, unable to allow my face to show any emotion. But then I saw it. Another cyclist. The second placed rider, coming round the final bend. I looked straight at my watch, fifty-five seconds. He was only fifty-five seconds behind. By the time he crossed the line, the gap had grown slightly to fifty-nine seconds. I was furious. Coppi would have won by ten or fifteen minutes from the same position, but I had lost my grip on reality. This was not Coppi, this was an eighteen year old boy, but it was too late, I had to teach him a lesson. He had to learn that winning was not enough, he had to win by more. So, I marched straight over to my son, and slapped him in front of everyone. Then I shouted at him that he had no right to celebrate because he had slacked off going up the hill. No champion would ever do that, and he would learn that lesson today. I swept up his bike and threw it into the back of my wagon, and ordered him inside. I turned, and drove straight back down the way I'd just come, to the foot of the mountain, where the race was still in progress for the many stragglers just reaching the climb.'

My dad seemed to be just staring into nowhere, no doubt remembering the pain and embarrassment he must have felt at the time.

'Then,' my grandfather continued, his voice cracking with emotion, 'I made him get on his bike and ordered him to do it again. He begged and begged me not to – he'd just won the race, he cried at me – I snapped back and told him that he didn't win it well enough, and threatened to hit him again if he didn't ride back up that mountain and raised my fist high to him. Another spectator, a father of another cyclist – a good man – came and told me to stop humiliating Luca, but I told him I would punch him in the face if he made another sound. He didn't. Then, with a smack of the back of my hand against your father's head, I forced him to ride. And through his tears, ride he did. He got back to the top of the mountain in just 37 minutes, he even finished before some of the riders in the original race. It was the bravest thing I had ever seen on a bike, not even Coppi had done anything so brave. It was the ride of a Champion. He was so tired at the top, but he never took his eyes off me. I can still see the hatred in them now. And that was the moment I knew I had lost my son. I wanted to tell him I was sorry, and that I had been so wrong, so ignorant and stupid, but my pride wouldn't allow that. So instead, like the coward that all bullies are, I just ignored him, placed his bike in the wagon and drove us home.'

I couldn't believe what I was hearing, but there was more to tell. My grandfather continued.

'In the morning, I got up to milk the cows and saw his bike, that bike, Danilo,' Grandpa said, pointing at the bike I had been riding for the past few days, now lying discarded on the gravel, 'leaning against the back of my wagon. I knew it was strange because it would usually be in the barn. Then I noticed the scratched metal on the frame. He had scraped off his name, the biggest insult any cyclist can give to a coach, scrape off your name and hand him back your empty bike. My son could take no more. I had broken him and he left here. And the shame has burned my soul ever since. The next time I saw him was this week, with you, Danilo. Twenty years. Twenty years without my son, all because I was an ignorant fool.'

For a while, there was nothing. Total silence. Nothing from my father, nothing from my grandfather and certainly nothing from me.

After what seemed ages, my grandfather broke the silence and looked directly at my father.

'Some people say that sorry is the hardest word to say Luca. But for me, it is by far the easiest. I have said sorry to your memory every day for the past twenty years. As much as I have dreaded this day, so I have welcomed it. I know you may never believe me, but I only wanted you to make the most of your ability Luca, it was just that I was too stupid to realise that you didn't need me – you didn't need anyone. The same as Coppi. You could have done it all on your own. My curse, the curse I will carry for the rest of my days, is that I took a shining jewel, and turned it into nothing better than a dirty stone on this path,' he said kicking loose the gravel under his feet, 'but I also realise that nothing can ever change that now. Those mistakes are made and are final. You never cycled again and I ruined your relationship with your son. I cannot believe I have caused so much sorrow, and I don't even ask for your forgiveness. I just say sorry. I love you and I respect you for your strength, your determination and the love that you have for your son. Now that I have told you these things, I will be able to face the rest of my life with some content-ment. I will always regret our lost years, and maybe this too will be the last time we speak. But I am just glad I have been able to say these things to you, along with one final thing.'

He moved toward my father before stopping. Then he said quietly, looking my father directly in his eyes.

'You did nothing wrong Luca. You did nothing wrong ... ever.'

At this, my father broke down and wept, before turning and walking into the house. For him now, it was over. Finally.

I looked at my grandfather, now broken too, and didn't know what to say. I simply didn't know. So I just turned away from him, saying nothing, and walked into the house to see my father.

The father I now knew I loved more than I ever had before.

20

WE sat on the bed and looked at each other, then at the packed suit-cases that lay between us. All the tears were dry, it was early evening and Dad had announced to me quite calmly that we were going to a hotel for the night, and then we were going to catch a flight the following afternoon back to Cardiff. He just wanted to tell his mother first.

'So you'll get to see Jamie soon after all,' he smiled.

But I was the one looking grumpy at the thought of going home early now.

'This is wrong,' I said finally, breaking the awkward silence that had lasted too long.

'Wrong, what do you mean wrong?' asked my dad.

'Dad, I used to hate you.' I said firmly. 'Even up to three days ago, I used to hate you. Then, when I was out cycling with Grandpa, he began to turn me around. Everything he said about you was good. He said how strong you are, how kind you are and how much respect he has for you. The love in his voice when he spoke about you, started to make me realise that I was being stupid in my hatred of you. Now that I know the truth about the reasons why you hated cycling, and the pain you have experienced in your life, I realise how stupid and how spoilt I've been. What type of person would I be, if now knowing the truth, I still hated you? I would be a buffoon. And that's what you will be if you leave here now without at least trying to rebuild things with your father.'

'Are you calling me a buffoon Dan?' asked my father in mock annoyance.

'Yes I am,' I replied, laughing. After a moment, I was serious again.

'What Grandpa did to you was horrible. I have no idea what that must have been like. But I've spent the last few days with him and I know that the horrible, spiteful man that you remember does not exist anymore. He is a fantastic teacher of cycling – you should hear him – he knows everything. But above all he only encourages, and does not push. He just guides me and allows me to take his advice or not. He's just kept on and on to me to try to be the best that I can be, but allows me to work out what that means for me myself ... not him. Those aren't the words of a bully, those are the words of someone who cares. Someone who loves.'

My dad sat in silence looking at me. I think he felt proud. It was odd for me too. It was the most grown up I'd ever felt. As if I'd suddenly matured that very afternoon.

A cliché I know, but I felt that in witnessing such an extraordinary scene involving the two men closest to me biologically, I had turned into a man.

'Dad, more than anything else, I want to be a cyclist. I am absolutely certain about this now, and I'm sure at some point, you must have wanted to do exactly that too. I just happen to be a kid who has a father who was apparently the best cyclist Italy had since Fausto Coppi and a grandfather who spent twelve years cycling alongside him. That's a hell of an advantage for me to take into the next round Gower sponsored cycle race for under-sixteens.'

My father laughed out loud at that point, 'You certainly size situations up well Dan, I'll give you that. So what are you saying to me?'

'Let's stay' I pleaded. 'Please. What would be the point of leaving? I know that your father did terrible things to you and I know it must still hurt – but the most important thing is that he knows that now too. He knew it then, but his pride got in the way. I just think it would be a real shame if you lost each other again, especially just as I am finding you both. What's done is done. He knows you will never forgive him and in a funny way, I don't think he wants you to. But now you know all the facts, you also know that he started out by doing what he really did think was the very best for you. Not for him, for you. He just got it wrong, that's all, horribly wrong and it just got too big for him to control. Sadly, you paid a terrible price for that.'

I paused again, quite surprised once more about where these mature words were coming from – I clearly was starting to grow up – but I wasn't going to stop now ... I was on a roll.

'I just think that now you know the truth, the least you can do is give it the rest of the three weeks and see if you can build some sort of a relationship with him. That's what I want to do with you. I love Jamie, but I want to stay here with you until the end of the holiday now, not go home. Me, you and Grandpa all have this one final chance to come together forever. It would be stupid to walk away now.'

'What, stupid like a buffoon?' my father said with a smile.

'Yes, a great big stupid buffoon,' I laughed.

21

✻

THE following morning during breakfast, Dad explained everything in Italian to my grandmother who kept kissing her rosary throughout, until the very end, when I'm guessing he told her that we were staying after all, at which point she burst into tears – for once of joy – and delivered him one of her rib crunching hugs. Then, looking at me, I could tell what was coming. This time I was ready, braced myself and squeezed her back with all my might.

After breakfast, Dad went to get his father, and when he found him, he called me outside to join them both. My grandfather looked very nervous, but I had guessed what was coming.

'Ok. After yesterday, I don't think any of us want a big speech,' said my dad, 'so I'll keep this short. Papa, do you know who the wisest one of the three of us is?'

'Yes I do Luca, I have known all along. It is this man here,' he said, ruffling my hair.

'Correct,' said my dad.

I was officially the complete opposite of gutted.

'He has made things very clear to me. One of the clearest things, is that the past should remain where it is ... in the past'

'I am so sorry Luca, please beli...'

My father stopped him with a swish of his hand. Where had I seen that before? I smiled to myself.

'Papa, we said all we needed to say yesterday – it is all in the past now. Agreed?'

'Yes Luca' said my grandfather, awkwardly offering his hand to my father.

My father paused, looking at this old, gnarled, hardworking hand, before looking up, deep into his father's eyes. Then, following the pause, he took the outstretched hand, grasping it with a vice-like grip. The handshake led to a hug, which I was subsequently dragged into. Then, after a brief tearful moment, it was over.

'Ok,' said my father dabbing his eyes. 'Today, I want to do something I have never done before in my life. I want to go cycling with my son.'

'Ah! Beautiful!' exclaimed my grandpa. 'That is wonderful! You must take my bike, I am so pleased!'

'I can't use your bike,' said my father sternly, and as he did, my grandfather's face dropped to his boots.

'Ok my son, I understand,' he muttered in embarrassment, probably realising my father could not bear to touch it.

'No you don't actually,' said my father smiling. 'I can't use your bike because you'll be riding it.'

My grandfather looked as happy as anyone I'd ever seen. He walked forward slowly, stopped and simply touched my father's face and said quietly: 'Thank you Luca. Thank you.'

'What are you going to ride then, Dad?' I asked.

'Oh, I think your grandfather will have something in that barn that I can borrow.'

'Yes, I still have them all Luca,' Grandpa smiled.

'One last thing Papa.' My grandfather stopped and looked at Dad as he spoke. 'There is one thing I do want to hear about from the past again, as much for me as Danilo to be honest.'

'What's that?' my grandfather asked.

'Coppi. Tell us about Coppi. I want to hear the stories again, and if this boy here wants to be a cyclist, he needs to learn everything there is to know about him'

'Oh, I will tell him,' promised my grandfather. 'I will tell you both, but let's get these bikes sorted first, and Danilo, you go and get changed.'

22

SOON, we were all out on the road, and to be honest, it was slightly awkward at first. I was being over friendly with Dad, Dad was being over-friendly with Grandpa and Grandpa was being over-friendly with everyone. But quickly we settled into a nice gentle rhythm out on the road, when Dad turned to Grandpa and said, pointing at me: 'You were right Papa, the boy has talent, very smooth. I should have noticed before. Is he as good as I was?'

'Easily,' said my grandfather, seriously.

'Bloody hell,' I said loudly, 'and you were supposed to be better than Coppi.' Both of them laughed instead of giving me a slap for swearing.

'Tell the boy about Coppi's first Milan – San Remo,' said my father. 'He needs to understand that first.'

'The day the legend was born,' nodded my grandfather. 'Yes, the perfect place. Danilo, we have spoken many times about the Tour de France, yes?'

'We have,' I agreed cheerfully.

'Well, do you really know what it is made up of?'

'I think so,' I replied confidently, 'twenty-one stages, with two rest days, some flat and some mountain stages too. It's really hard.'

'Yes it is my boy,' he said, 'it is over two thousand miles these days, longer in Coppi's time of course, but it is called a Grand Tour. Similar races are the Giro d'Italia, which is our own Grand Tour here in Italy, and the Spanish version, the Vuelta. Now, there are many other smaller tours, but after the Grand Tours, a cyclist who wants to become a great, will try to win one of the Classics. Have you heard of these boy?'

'No.' I replied.

'I thought not,' he smiled. There are several Classics. The Paris-Roubaix in France, The Fleche Wallone in Belgium and the Liege-Bastogne-Liege also held in Belgium. But there is one that stands above them all, and it has been run on these very roads. It is the Milan – San Remo. There are only three things you really need to know about that race. First, it is the longest of all the Classics at one hundred and eighty-five miles in total. Second it is Italy's favourite race bar none – if a non-Italian wins it, the country goes into mourning, and third, one man won it three times in four years straight after the war finished, do you know who that was?'

'Coppi?'

'Of course Coppi,' laughed my grandfather, 'and the first time he won it, it created a legend that just grew and grew and lives on to this very day. It was not long after Fausto and me had met on these roads when I was that angry young man. About a week before the race he had said to me 'I shall win the *La Primavera* next week Umberto my friend'. I just laughed and told him of course he would. But then he shot an icy glance at me and said, 'Believe me Umberto this is no joke, and I shall not just win, I shall crush them all, and I will do it for all of Italy. I will be first home in San Remo.' To this very moment, as much as he personally had to gain from victory, I honestly still believe that he wanted to win this race, not just for the riches and fame it might have brought him, but mainly because he knew that our country needed a hero to believe in after the war had robbed us of our hope and our pride. Fausto wanted to be that hero. I knew even back then, that when Fausto set his mind on something, he would usually achieve it. If ever you leave this country and live out your dreams as a cyclist, Danilo, it would be my dream to see you back here as a grown man and win the Milan-San Remo like Coppi did.'

'Anyway,' continued my grandfather, after a brief pause of reflection, 'just as he said to me a week before, not only did he win, he crushed them. Importantly, it was his first race as leader of the Bianchi team. Before the war he had been the joint leader of the Legnano team, but the rivalry he had with that other great Italian champion, Gino Bartali, not only divided the team, it divided the whole of Italy. Amongst all the other reasons Fausto had for winning, was a very selfish one, he also wanted to humiliate Bartali. One thing that everyone knew about the Milan - San Remo is that because it was such a long race, an early break would be suicide if you really wanted to win it. So what did Coppi do? He made an early break!' my grandfather chuckled and shook his head at the memory.

'The man that went with him was Teisseire, the champion of France, and Bartali just sat there in the bunch and let them both go, so certain was he that they would be caught in time, probably laughing at the foolishness of the inexperienced Coppi. But Bartali himself had made one critical mistake. The route went right past Fausto's front door. There is a mountain over there called 'The Turchino' and it was on its slopes that Bartali planned to catch him, but he never got close. Fausto had made that climb a thousand times – many of them with me – and he just left them all on the climb, and eventually emerged from the famous tunnel at the top, to the absolute delight of all the tifosi – the fans – who waited for him. Way out in front and almost unrecognisable caked as he was in dust, muck, and sweat. Still, they all still knew it was Coppi from his unmistakable smooth style, and every single one of them went mad. He descended from the mountain like an eagle, or more accurately a Heron, which was one of his many nicknames, and swept to victory along the coast in San Remo a full fourteen minutes ahead of the Frenchman Teisseire. It was truly an amazing victory, destroying as he did, the strongest field to assemble in a race since before the War. The final humiliation though was for Bartali, the crowds at the finish had to wait another ten minutes after Teisseire for the great former Italian champion. This proud man was so angry, he didn't even stop at the finish line, he just carried on straight back to his hotel in silence, acknowledging no one. Fausto had crushed them all, in the most spectacular style, and his legend was born. People still talk of it today as the race that changed all of Italy.'

I looked at my father who seemed totally absorbed by the story, even though he must have heard it a hundred times. My grandfather was silent too, he was probably back in his youth, thinking of the times when he rode with Coppi at pace, not trundling along the roads with a kid like me. I glanced ahead, along our long flat road, and looked up toward the mountains ahead, in the direction that my grandfather had pointed when he spoke of Coppi's climb up the Turchino. And I made myself a promise there and then ... I would come back here and take part in that race. The Milan – San Remo. I may never win it, but I would give my all to come back here to compete in it, a fitting present to give to my grandfather.

'Grandpa, you mentioned his breakaway was suicide. How long was he out in front of the others?'

'One hundred and sixteen miles,' both men answered together.

'When I was a child growing up in school,' said my father turning to me, 'one of the very first things we were all taught about was the details of that great victory and the huge effect it had on the Italian people. It is the one single moment that made me know that I wanted to be a cyclist like my father. Like Coppi.'

'And so do I,' I said under my breath, 'so do I.'

23

❊

THE next day my grandfather was feeling the effects of our few days of cycling, bearing in mind he hadn't been on a bike for twenty years before this week, and as delighted as he was to be back on terms with his son, I think he was happy to rest his legs for the day. No such luck for me though! My dad had seen my face light up yesterday when I had been listening to the story of Coppi leaving everyone behind on the slopes of the Turchino, so after breakfast, he asked if I wanted to see it. I instantly agreed, but was a bit worried that it was too far.

'We'll be going by car Dan, you buffoon,' he said laughing at the relief on my face. 'We'll borrow Papa's pick up and put the bikes in the back, then I'll drive you half way up and we'll see if we can't get you up to the top from there.'

About an hour later, Dad pulled the pick up into a lay-by about halfway up the mountain. It was quite a bleak hill, very brown in colour, the road dusty from the lack of rainfall in this typically hot Italian summer. I was quite nervous, and Dad could tell.

'Don't worry Dan,' he encouraged. 'I've come a little higher than halfway. It's about nine miles in total, but we've got about four to do. Just do it as best you can, you'll be fine.'

'The best that I can be, Dad?'

'Yes,' he laughed, 'the best that you can be', adding quietly, 'that's all I'll ever ask of you.'

Dad locked the car, put the keys in his pocket and off we went. The road to the right was bounded by the mountain, the road to the left was bounded by a wall, with the mountainside below it seeming to drop down for miles. I gulped.

Soon, we had found a decent rhythm and were climbing quite

easily. Where I was positioned, less than a wheel length behind my dad, I could see what my grandfather had meant when he said my dad was a natural when we were having the big argument. I had never seen somebody handle a bike so smoothly. I tried to copy everything he did. He didn't talk much as he went, he just kept glancing back every minute or so and asking me if I was ok. I had never felt better. Yes, my legs ached the higher we went, but not all parts were steep and Dad had the knack of finding the flattest bits of the climb the further we went. I stuck to him like glue. Every time he stood up out of the saddle, so did I. Every time he sat back down and changed gear, so did I. I wiped my brow the same time that he did, I threw the sweat away and spat the same time he did, and I took a drink the same time he did and the joy I had from being on this mountain – as hard as it was – and copying my father knew no bounds. All those days of hate, of wishing I was back home without him, of just wishing he wasn't in my life, were banished forever on that mountain, such was the respect I had for his cycling ability, and the love I now had for him as a dad. As we reached the mountain's summit I could see the tunnel, I was tired now, really tired and my legs were screaming with the build up of the lactic acid in them, but all I could hear was my grandfather's soft voice 'Be the best you can be Danilo, the best you can be.' The energy I gained from his voice pushed me up alongside my father, instead of being stuck behind his wheel. He looked at me with genuine surprise.

'The tunnel,' I panted, and gestured with my head, let's go through, like Coppi.'

'Ok.' He smiled. 'Ok.'

So, onward and upward we went until we reached the tunnel. It was much shorter than I thought it would be, less that a hundred yards long, but all I could think of as I tasted the dust from the mountain that filled my mouth from the ride up, was Coppi, flying out in a cloud of this same dust, to the cheers of all the Italian fans. As we emerged into the sunlight, I tried to imagine the scene that would have greeted him, but in all honesty, I couldn't. I knew I needed to learn more about this man. He was the key. If I could devote myself to Coppi, then perhaps I could someday race like he had done, on the roads that he had cycled with my grandfather.

'Dad. I'm telling you now,' as we leant against our bikes at the top of the Turchino, slurping greedily from our water bottles after we had stopped and dismounted, 'I'm going to come back here someday, and I'm going to come out of that tunnel just as he did. I promise you.'

My dad just looked back at me, before he said, 'Well, if you want it enough, you will. But that is what you need Dan, the hunger. Despite what Grandpa did to me, I never had it, it was never within me. I was good, yes, but cycling to me was never the be all and end all of my life. Even if Grandpa hadn't treated me that way, I don't think there would have been much difference. It was just something I was good at, I didn't love it enough.'

'I do, Dad. I want to learn everything I can to get me there. I want to know the best way to ride, the quickest way to ride, when I should eat and when I should drink and when I should rest. I want to learn about Coppi, I want to learn about how he won races and I want to know how he managed to crush his opponents.' I was now speaking as fast as my grandmother and continued: 'I want to know what it was like to live like him and train like him. I want to know about tactics and how make breakaways.' I stopped for a moment, thinking of the right phrase to explain what was in my mind. 'Dad, I want to learn how to be a professional – it's as simple as that.'

'Then there is only one person to teach you.' My father paused for a moment, then smiled and shook his head as he looked out over the spectacular view from the top of 'Coppi's Mountain'. 'I can't believe I'm about to say this as I never, ever thought that I would utter these words, but the very best person to teach you is my father. He holds all the keys to your dreams.'

24

*

THE next ten days were, as I look back now with total certainty, the best and most important ten days of my life, not to mention some of the happiest. In a strange way the cycling was insignificant. Yes, I covered plenty of miles with my dad and started to build the body – and legs – I would need to allow me to compete in the professional ranks. And yes, it was then that I developed my style, a carbon copy of my dad's, with his smooth, fast leg speed or cadence as my grand-father kept telling me. But it was in conversation with my grandfather where I began to grow as a person. He knew so much about life, respect and honour, that he totally began to change my outlook on life. I began to realise what a selfish and self centred person I had been up to that point of my life. He explained how I had to under-stand that for any cyclist to be successful he has to give all of himself – one hundred per cent – to his team. It is only once this has been understood and done consistently, then recognised by your team-mates that they will return the favour and ride for you on the day that possible race victory comes knocking on your door. I had no idea up to then how teamwork was absolutely key to victory in professional cycling. But what helped more than anything, what made me absorb these important lessons better than I could have ever hoped, was that my grandfather knew so much about Coppi, that he had a story to illustrate every situation and lesson that he was teaching me. It was so much easier to learn when somebody painted a picture as clearly as my grandfather was able to, by using Coppi as his canvas.

Two days after my trip over the top of the Turchino with my dad, I was told by both him and Grandpa to have a rest day. Rest, they both said, was as important as exercise in the life of any sportsman, not just a cycling. They didn't get too many arguments from me because my legs were feeling as though they had lead, not blood running through them that morning when I got up, so I just busied myself by simply strolling round the farm in the sun. After about ten minutes, when I was going over in my mind all the incredible events that I had witnessed and experienced in the past days, I remembered something Grandpa had said on the morning that Dad and him had buried the hatchet, the day following the big row. It was when Dad had said that Grandpa would probably be able to find a spare bike for him, and he'd replied with a huge smile: 'Yes, I still have them all Luca.' I was so happy at the time, that I paid no attention to his remark. But now that I had time to think, I decided that I wanted to see what 'them all' meant.

I headed straight to the barn and walked inside. As dark as usual, it took a few moments for my eyes to adjust again. I looked around, and the unbelievable collection of tools and equipment seemed exactly the same as they had been when I walked in there, snooping around, that very first time ten days before. There, in the corner, under its tarpaulin was 'my' bike, lying idle. As untidy as the barn was, strangely, nothing actually looked out of place. But still there was no obvious signs of any other bikes, apart from mine.

Slowly, I looked around and walked to each corner, scanning the walls closely as I went, but there was nothing. I was totally stumped. I went into the other barns, but they were only used for storage of the tractors and trailers that Grandpa used on the farm, and there was nothing stored in any that compared to the amount of equipment in the main barn. That left the last building, the smallest and most run down of them all. I walked in but this building didn't even have a roof, and apart from some old milking equipment, there was nothing else in there. Frustrated, I went back into the first barn, and just sat down in the middle of the floor, on some straw. Where could these bikes be? I kept thinking. Then I had a light bulb moment. I thought back to that time when Grandpa had caught me in there, when I returned the bike after that first time out on the roads, and I was trying to get the tarpaulin back over it. From memory, I remembered that he'd been standing somewhere, somewhere where I couldn't see him. I then remembered thinking at the time – after I'd jumped out of my skin – that he couldn't have followed me in, as I'd have heard him. My light bulb moment was to realise that perhaps he was in there already!

I tried to remember exactly where my grandfather was standing when he gave me the fright, and I decided it was by the opposite wall to my bike, just below the high window and next to the set of open cupboards that held so many of the old farming tools in racks. And then I saw it. The cupboard was not set back flush against the wall, instead it was about three feet forward of it, leaving a gap behind it. I walked up to this cupboard and poked my head behind it, and, surprise, surprise there was a door. It was almost completely hidden from view in the darkness, and was closed.

I was just about to open it, and then I remembered how annoyed Grandpa had been when I'd opened his trunk, so I pulled back. 'No,' I thought to myself, 'you're not that kid any more, go and ask him for permission to go in there like a grown up would do'. I was quite enjoying being the new, responsible me.

So, I walked back outside, looked down to the logs where I thought Grandpa would be, and there he was, sitting, drinking a glass of lemonade. He turned when he heard my footsteps approaching.

'Danilo my boy, it is you ... how are those legs today – tired? Rest is often the best form of training, come, sit with me. We still have plenty to talk about.'

'Yes, I will soon Grandpa, but I've got something to ask you first.'

'Oh? What is it my boy, you can asked me anything,' he smiled.

'Well, it's the barn. You know that first day you caught me in there with the bike?'

'Yes,' he replied cautiously.

'Well, I couldn't work out why I hadn't heard you coming in.'

'That's very true,' he nodded. 'I think you might have just found out about my secret room, am I right?'

'Yes,' I blushed, before quickly adding, 'I wasn't snooping mind, and I didn't go in, I ... I just wanted to see if you had bikes in there.'

My grandfather laughed. 'Come on, I was going there soon anyway,' and he got up, grabbed my arm and led me to the barn. Once there he walked straight to the cupboard, slipped behind it, and opened the door. I heard the clunk of the lock, followed by the click of the light, and then he called me in. 'Come Danilo, welcome to my workroom.'

I walked in and I just found myself rooted to the spot. Inside were about fifteen racing bikes of different styles and ages. Many were hanging from frames on the ceiling, some were attached to the walls and two – his and the one my dad had been using – were up on stands in the middle of the room, next to a work bench.

'Those two need a clean, it was going to my job for the morning. And now you can help me,' he laughed.

'Whose bikes are these?' I asked stupidly.

'Well they are mine of course' and he made a cross eyed look of a fool mocking me, exposing the gap in his teeth which made him look even more comical. I blushed and giggled which made him laugh more.

He gave me a tour of all the bikes, from the earliest one he ever had, the one he'd been riding when he nearly crashed into Coppi all those years before, through to his first professional bike, to the ones toward the end of his career when the iconic Bianchi blue colour first appeared on the frames, right up to the three he had built for my father in preparation for him joining a professional team.

'Do you know Danilo, between 1930 and 1980, bikes hardly changed. Most were made of butted steel, and then simply painted in a single colour. The tubes of the frames were joined together by these lugs and were then soldered together tight. Easy really. The principal for building them never changed, and so long as the steel was strong, and that you looked after it and cleaned it, then there was no reason why your bike couldn't last you a lifetime. This one here,' he patted the saddle of the one he'd been riding with me, 'I built this for my final season – 1959 – but sadly, due to my injuries, I never got to ride it in a race. It is still as good as new.'

I looked closely at it and it was absolutely immaculate, a thing of beauty.

'Of course, it was all then spoiled by your friend Mr Boardman!' he said in mock anger. 'You see, he knew the secret was weight. These old steel bikes were perfect to ride, strong, durable, comfortable, but they were heavy. And let me tell you, the last thing you need when you are trying to cycle up an Alp is a heavy bike! This bike probably weighs nearly thirty pounds in weight. Now, thanks to Mr Boardman and his carbon fibre machines, the professional bikes can weigh as little as fifteen pounds. Amazing. Mind you, they are not as comfortable as these bikes,' he said, still patting the leather saddle of his old favourite. 'All these bikes represent my life's work you know, they are priceless to me which is why I have hidden this room and kept it locked when I am not here. It is the place where I like to spend most of my time. Each bike has different memories for me, magical memories. Many of your brilliant father.'

We spent the rest of the morning cleaning the two bikes he'd put on the stands, which did not just mean wiping them over with an oily rag as I had thought, instead we basically took them apart, pedals, chains, brakes, gears everything. I had absolutely no idea what I was doing, but I loved every second of it.

'Even the very best cyclist has to be a great mechanic,' he told me. You can be stranded anywhere – even when you are a pro – and you must know your bike inside and out in order to fix it. Sometimes you will be alone, without a team mate and with your team car servicing one of your colleagues. You must be able to then do as much of the repairs as you can manage. It can sometimes be the difference between winning and losing.'

As we were packing everything away, he asked me to fetch him an air pressure gauge from one of the two trunks at the side of his work bench to see how much air was in the tyres of the two bikes we'd dismantled, cleaned, then put back together again. I didn't listen clearly to his instruction, and went into the wrong trunk. It didn't seem to have any tools in it, just a lot of beige clothing. I laughed. It was where he kept all his old riding kit. I reached inside to try to find the black beret he wore, so that I could put it on and have a laugh with him. But as I was rooting around, something caught my eye. Something in bright yellow. My heart stopped for a moment. It couldn't be could it? Not a yellow jersey?

I stopped and spun round at him straight away, I didn't want another row. He was looking straight at me, but this time, not with anger, but with pride.

'It is ok, Danilo, you can bring it out. It has been a very long time.'

I turned back, looked down into the trunk and moved his beige training gear, dropping his beret on the floor as I did so. Just as I was about to pull out the jersey, Dad popped his head in and called: 'Ah, I thought I might find you two in here, what are you doing?'

I stopped immediately – forgetting for a moment that all was now well between Dad and Grandpa.

'It's ok, Danilo,' Grandpa said. 'Bring it out. I have never shown this to Luca before, I was saving it for a day that never came.' He turned to my dad: 'Come, Luca, please, let me show you this. One day I had hoped to give this to you.'

I pulled the jersey out of the trunk, held it up and it unravelled before me. It was magical. It made the jerseys I'd found in Grandpa's trunk in the bathroom look like old sacks of potatoes. It was incredibly striking. My father just gasped when he realised what it was.

'Papa – that wasn't yours was it?' he asked in awe, pointing at the jersey open-mouthed.

'Well, yes and no Luca, yes and no.'

I was transfixed by the beauty of this jersey, the absolute pinnacle of professional cycling. Even at my young age, thanks to the obsession Jamie and I had shared for the Tour de France, I knew how valuable the yellow jersey of the Tour de France was. This version was very similar to the style of the jerseys I had already seen in Grandpa's trunk, and it was clearly very old. It was made of wool, short sleeved and had two buttons leading up to the huge collars that flopped towards the floor as I held it up. In front, along the top of the pockets were the words BIANCHI, this time much smaller than I'd seen on the other jerseys, and not sewn on as perfectly, almost as if they were a late addition to it. Underneath it and on the right hand pocket below the button, was a weird squiggle which looked like a letter 'H' interwoven with an upside down 'D'.

'What does that mean, Grandpa,' I asked, as I ran my fingers over its thick black embroidery which made the letters stand proud of the surface of the jersey.

'That is the signature of the man that created the Tour De France in 1903, Henri Desgrange. His signature appears on every yellow jersey that is awarded – even to this very day. Your friend Big Mig will have seen that signature many times.'

'But Papa,' interrupted my dad, 'this jersey – is it yours or not.'

'Well, it is mine Luca, but,' he paused, 'I didn't win it. Although, the circumstances of my receiving it mean more to me that had I actually won it myself. Let me explain. It was the 1952 Tour de France, the last of Fausto's two great victories in that legendary race. It was the morning of the ninth stage, and on the morning, Fausto called us together – his 'Gregari', the men who surround their leader and try to deliver him the ultimate victory in Paris by the end of the Tour. The instruction he gave us that morning in Mulhouse, was that myself and our great friend, the loyal workhorse Andrea Carrea, were to make sure that we went with any breakaway that any other riders attempted. Fausto would make sure that he would stay with the leader of the race at the time, a fellow Italian named Fiorenza Magni, who proudly wore the yellow, and make sure, it was not him but Coppi himself that wore the yellow jersey by the end of the day. All went well to begin with, and Carrea and myself went with the first early break, expecting the peloton – including Coppi – to catch us quite soon. This would then enable Coppi to make a break of his own much later, which would leave Magni stranded, delivering the yellow jersey to Coppi, our 'Patron'. That was our plan. The trouble was, the men in the breakaway pedalled like demons. Carrea and I had no option but to sit in behind them and wait for them to burn themselves out. It never happened.'

'Did you get the yellow jersey Grandpa?' I asked excitedly.

'No, I did not. That dubious honour fell to the faithful Carrea. It absolutely broke his heart.'

'Broke his heart?' I exclaimed. 'I don't understand. He wanted to lead the race surely?'

'No my boy, that is the whole point. The likes of Carrea and me were gregari, we were not there to win or lead races, that was not our job. We were the soldiers of the Patron, our leader Coppi. In France they are called domestiques.'

He continued to explain. 'Domestiques exist to help, protect and do everything they can to deliver victory for the Patron, the name we have in Italy for the team leader. There were times in my career when I gave my bike to Fausto, leaving myself stranded and would walk fifty miles if it meant him finishing and winning. And I did this for him with delight, with pride. I was his gregario. All of us were the same, as long as we helped Fausto to win that is all that mattered. The thought of us winning instead of him never crossed our minds. In fact, to do so would be the ultimate shame, the ultimate dishonour.'

I tried to understand this loyal approach and mentioned to my grandfather that teamwork seemed to be the most important part of cycling.

'Absolutely my little Danilo. You understand perfectly. You look at the long list of winners of the Tour de France from the day that Mr Desgrange invented it and I will tell you this with certainty, none of them, not even Coppi himself, could possibly have won without their many gregari – it is simply not possible. Many times the race has been won by the Patron of the best team, not necessarily by the best rider in the race.'

'I still don't understand why your friend Carrea was so upset at wearing the yellow jersey though?'

'Because he felt that he had humiliated his Patron, and in so doing brought terrible shame on himself. I remember it so well. We were cycling into Lausanne in Switzerland, and the finish was no more than four miles away. It was clear now that the main bunch were not going to catch us, so the stage winner was going to come from one of the eight of us in the breakaway. I was never a sprinter, whereas Carrea had the heart of a lion, so I told him to stick with the leaders of the group and make sure that if they sprinted, he would stick with them and finish with the same time as them. But Carrea knew that because his time on the Tour was so good that year, it would mean that the time he gained from Fausto – which on this stage would prove to be over nine minutes – would be enough to not just take the yellow jersey from Magni, but also place it on his own back, instead of it going onto the shoulders of our patron, Coppi. In terms of cycling honour, it would appear to everyone else to be the most obvious betrayal and humiliation of Coppi, as if Carrea had intended to be the leader of the race – and maybe the team. Even if Carrea won the stage, well, that would be one thing, but to take yellow in front of his Patron would be unforgivable. As it turned out, there was no sprint, Carrea stuck to his task and he and I crossed the line together with the same time as the stage winner, Walter Diggelmann – seven hours, twenty-three minutes and sixteen seconds. This meant that the nine minutes that Carrea had taken from our Patron, Coppi, saw Carrea become the leader of the Tour de France, and was therefore awarded the yellow jersey, but to his absolute horror!'

'But I knew the full story, and betrayal and humiliation had nothing to do with the position Carrea now found himself in. He had got there because he had done what he always did, a loyal, professional job, simply following the orders he was given. But, still, no matter that he knew this himself, Carrea was distraught. He was a man who lived his whole life with honour – he still does – and he was terrified that people may really believe that he had engineered his high finish to shame his Patron. He was so upset that he was actually about to get off as we rode closer to the line and wait for Coppi on the roadside, but I barked at him not to do such a thing, that he should carry on and get the best possible time on the stage for Italy.'

'So is that what he did?' asked my father.

'Yes. And that decision meant that he would take the leader's yellow jersey. But my good friend Carrea couldn't bear the shame. When they presented him with the leader's jersey on the podium in the stadium, he was in floods of tears, so humiliated that he had somehow deceived and let down his Patron in such a public way. When he eventually went to Fausto to explain, he continued to cry like a baby apologising and saying he had no right to wear the jersey that only belonged to his Captain.'

'What did Coppi say?' I asked

'Well, to be honest with you, at first even I feared he would be angry, so important was the yellow jersey – but I knew him so well, that I couldn't believe that was how he really felt. Instead, he was genuinely touched by the tears of Carrea, and realised once again, with Carrea's public outpouring of grief, that he had people around him that would do anything for him. He then went straight to the assembled reporters and told them that he was delighted that Carrea, the most loyal of gregari, would experience the rare joy of the taste of triumph and success.'

My father and I looked at each other in silence, quite moved by the circumstances of this never before heard story.

My grandfather continued, 'The next day, was the first ever day that the riders of the Tour de France climbed possibly the greatest peak of them all, L'Alpe d'Huez. Coppi said little that morning, but it was clear, he wanted to win this new, challenging stage, and win it well. I also knew that it would again have to be me and Carrea to accompany the Patron that day as climbing was our speciality. Our loyal friend Carrea set off at the head of the peloton that morning, in so doing, becoming the first man ever to cycle that great Alp in the yellow jersey of a Champion. As the hours passed by and we approached the great Alp, I struggled on, and stayed with Fausto as

143

long as I could. The two of us were really flying that day and I led him out for as far as I could, until he left me, like the majestic climber he was, on that huge mountain. He won of course, chasing down and passing the breakaway Frenchman, Robic, and took the yellow jersey for himself. There was good news for me too, because Robic had the misfortune to suffer a puncture and because his team car was so far behind, he lost minutes trying to fix it, which meant that I managed to finish runner up for the second day running, which pleased me greatly. I stood and admired with happiness, my Captain placing the leader's jersey on his back, that he would now wear all the way to Paris and victory. He was never headed in the race again.'

My grandfather paused, his face a picture of contentment as he remembered these great days of his youth. My father and I just smiled at each other. After a moment, Grandpa began again.

'A week after the tour, I was in this very workshop when I heard a familiar voice. It was Coppi. I often repaired frames for him so it was no surprise to see him. He had a small brown paper parcel with him. He sat right there where you are sitting now Luca,' he said pointing at my father. 'He started talking about the Tour and how hard it was and how he didn't think that his body was strong enough to win another long Tour. He said he was happy now as he'd won it twice, and as he was 33, he knew that he wasn't getting any younger, so knew he wouldn't enter again. I told him not to be silly, he would win again – I really believed he would – but I also knew that he wasn't a well man, and the years of fatigue and pain had steadily taken their toll. Anyway, we chatted a little longer and he said to me something I shall never forget. He said 'Umberto my loyal friend, in all the time we have ridden you have never once won, am I right? I told him he was, and I told him that his victories were more than enough for me to feast on. He then said 'But in this Tour you came second on two successive days, on two of the hardest stages?' I replied that I did, but enjoyed every minute, and that was because he ended the Tour with his own deserved victory. My second places were immaterial as I had done my job. He just smiled, stood up and said 'Well, I shall never taste victory in that particular race again. But I want you to have this, because you deserved to taste it. Please open it when I have left.' 'Then we embraced, talked some more, but soon he was gone.'

All of a sudden, my grandfather went quiet and looked to the heavens as he often did when he told of his great friend. Then he spoke again, his voice cracking once again with emotion, preceding the tears that quickly came.

'And that is what was in the parcel Danilo,' sniffed my grandpa. 'That jersey you are now holding, the last yellow jersey 'Il Campionissimo' would ever wear in La Grand Boucle, and it has never left this room since.'

My father walked across and hugged his father. Again, Fausto Coppi was bringing this troubled family back together.

I concentrated on the jersey and held it softly, transfixed by it. Its beauty to me increased ten times now that I knew the story attached to it. My grandfather was right, it felt even better than if he had actually won it himself.

'He was a special man Papa,' said my father, finally breaking the silence.

'Yes he was Luca. A very, very special man.'

Getting up stiffly, my grandfather walked over to me, wiped his eyes, smiled and took the priceless yellow jersey from me, held it out in front of himself and took a long, hard, look at it. Then he turned to my father, walked across to him, embraced him, and handed him the jersey.

'So are you my son, so are you.'

25

THE following day, I was up early, rushed through breakfast and went straight to Grandpa's workshop where he was already working, an old bike in bits on the work bench in front of him, and about six tyre inner tubes draped over its edge, looking like a collection of dead eels awaiting gutting. I noticed that nearly every one of them had at least three or four patches on them. In his hands was another tube, to which he was applying some white glue from a scruffy glass pot, with what looked like an old toothbrush. I watched him for a moment as he put the brush back in the pot, sized, then cut a piece of rubber patching from a large sheet, tested that the glue was not too wet, then firmly pressed down the rubber patch over the glue. He held it in position for a minute or two, then draped it over the others that were already on the bench. He then picked up one he'd done earlier, grabbed some sandpaper and rubbed over the edges of a freshly applied patch until it was nice and smooth. Even though he was doing something relatively simple, just watching him was like seeing a master at work.

After a moment I spoke. 'Morning, Grandpa.'

'Morning Danilo, my boy,' he replied without even looking up. 'Have you come to give me a hand this morning,' he laughed. 'Are you ready for some hard work today?'

'Yes,' I replied, but I was hoping that the hard work would be out on the roads, not in here,' I said cheekily.

'I was only teasing you. We will wait for your father, and then decide where we are to go today.' I was thrilled by the thought.

As I continued to watch him work, I spoke.

'Grandpa, why do you repair so many tubes? Why don't you just buy replacements?'

'It is habit Danilo,' he replied. 'When I raced, the inner tube was your life line. Without three or four spares or the ability to repair them, you would have no chance of finishing a day out on the roads.'

'Why did you get so many punctures in those days then Grandpa,' I asked. 'I hardly ever get one.'

'It was the roads, boy. The roads when I raced were so much worse than they are today, especially in the mountains. The mountain passes in the Pyrenees and The Alps were nothing short of rugged tracks. When it rained, they turned to total mud baths, and these often hid the sharp stones that would give you punctures. It is only in recent years that they have been able to lay the smooth tarmac down on these high passes, which is the cyclists dream.'

I walked over and picked up three of the tubes. 'But how did you manage to carry three or four of these on the bike?' I asked, trying to work out the answer for myself.

'Your father has left the yellow jersey of Coppi in its box until you both fly home' said my grandfather pointing at the workbox. 'Go and fetch it back out and I will show you something you didn't notice yesterday.'

I didn't need a second invitation to seek out that fantastic piece of cycling history and soon it was in my hands. Just looking at it again just seemed to transmit some sort of magic feeling through my veins. I clearly wanted to get the chance of wearing one of these myself.

'Ok, now hold it out in front of you and tell me what you see.'

I looked at this wonderful piece of fabric, and tried to see something that I hadn't spotted yesterday. But I saw nothing.

'Hold it up to the light,' my grandfather suggested.

As I did I saw it, very faint, but it was there.

From each shoulder of the jersey on the front, in a kind of semi-circle that disappeared under the armpits on each side were two, inch wide, dark lines. The jersey had obviously been washed by Coppi before he presented it to my grandfather, but now as I held it to the light, I could see these two black lines, where dirt had been ground into the fabric so much, that the washing process hadn't quite got rid of these stains.

'Right, now turn it around, and hold it up to the light again.'

This I did, and now I could see similar dark lines on the back of the jersey, but this time they weren't straight, they were more like a figure of eight that crossed each other right in the middle of the shoulder blades.

'Those lines are caused by rubber being ground into our shoulders, chest and back, mixing with sweat and road dirt generated from eight hours a day on the bike,' he said.

'You carried your inner tubes around your shoulders?' I asked in wonder.

'Yes we did,' he replied. 'As I said, inner tubes were as important as oxygen to the professional cyclist. Without them, you were nothing. I witnessed many a man's dreams ending in tears on the slopes of the big climbs thanks to the razor sharp stones that would spike even the most tough rubber tyre, just as it happened to poor Robic to allow me second place on L'Alpe d'Huez. Anyway, every morning, each cyclist would have his breakfast, take on fluid, stretch his tired legs, check over his bikes, and then, the very last thing he would do before he climbed on his bike to start his race would be to tie on his inner tubes.'

'Wasn't it uncomfortable though, Grandpa?'

'The first time I did it, yes, but then it became as natural as putting on a cap. Once or twice, others would take the risk and not take any, and I never saw a time when that risk didn't end in tears. Me? I would never start a race without at least four. But it was always worth it. I tell you Danilo, one thing you never want to experience is the torture of climbing the highest mountain, only to be denied the delight of flying down the other side because you have no tyre!'

'What was it like climbing the highest mountains, Grandpa?' I asked.

'Mountains never held a fear for me Danilo, if I can be totally honest with you. For me, living around here with the mountains so close, they were just another obstacle to be dealt with. To those riders who lived around the flat plains of France or in the north or Europe, the mountains would play on their mind. They were often defeated before they even put a tyre on the smallest of slopes. A cyclist must learn to love the mountains and learn to respect them, it is only this way that you can finally defeat them. This is something I learned very early on with Fausto, and it is something you must learn too.'

I remembered the mixture of pain and elation that I felt just a few days previously with my father on the Turchino. I was beginning to understand what I was going to have to learn and undertake if I was ever going to achieve my dream of being a cyclist.

'Mind you,' said my grandfather, interrupting my thoughts, 'I was not so comfortable on the cobblestones. That was my great fear – The Hell of the North.'

'The Hell of the North?' I asked, 'What is that?'

'It was our name for a very important race,' replied my grandfather. 'Do you remember I mentioned the classics, the races that include our own Milan – San Remo?'

'Yes,' I replied. 'I told Dad the other day, that's the one race I want to compete in when I become a professional.'

'And I know you will do it Danilo, I know you will. But if you do achieve that, then one day you will also take part in The Hell of the North ... I wish you the best of luck with that,' said the old man, laughing.

'Why is it called Hell?' I asked.

'The cobbles. They provide the hell. The race is properly known as the Paris – Roubaix , the most demanding of all the races I ever took part in, but also one of the most prestigious in which to compete. The race began in Paris, then would run northwards to Roubaix which was close to the Belgian border. After the war, most of the roads out of Paris were not tarmac as they are today, but what the French call *pave,* which means cobblestones, which in turn translates to pain. You must wonder about my teeth Danilo,' my grandfather said, laughing, before giving me his fullest smile which showed how wonky and how many gaps he had in his teeth. 'Before I started the Hell of the North, my teeth were perfect and full – look what those cobblestones did to me, so much did they shake me to the bone!' Again he laughed out loud. 'We had to cover about one hundred and fifty miles on those infernal cobbles, cycling north through the old industrial areas of France, which meant another thing to add to your teeth being shaken out of your head – dirt, and lots of it. You learn to get used to everything as a cyclist Danilo, but the filth, mud, ash and grit that we would suffer in an inevitably wet April each year was torture. Give me a long steep mountain in the dry and heat any day. I just shudder when I remember this grueling race, but it did provide me with two everlasting memories of happiness. That was in 1949 and 1950, when the name of Coppi was engraved on the list of winners in consecutive years.'

'Gosh, he won a race as tough as that twice in a row Grandpa?'

'No, not quite. The name Coppi won it two years in succession, but Fausto only won one of them.'

'I don't understand,' I said.

'Fausto had a brother, Danilo, a brother called Serse. And it was dear Serse who was to break all of our hearts.'

26

❊

BEFORE Grandpa had chance to tell me about this revelation of Fausto having a brother who was also a cyclist, my grandmother came into the workshop and rattled off a list of demands for him, which saw him raising his eyes to the heavens.

'She wants me to go into town for some supplies,' he sighed, after my Grandmother had left, with me narrowly avoiding yet another crushing hug from her.

'That's ok,' I said happily. 'I can come can't I?'

'Yes of course,' my grandfather smiled, 'but I thought you would want to go out on the bike.'

'Yes, but Dad said he's got to make some phone calls to do with his next contract in work back home, so we can't go out until this afternoon, meaning I've got nothing else to do this morning anyway.'

'Ok my boy, that is very good news for me to have you along for the ride, I can tell you about dear, dear Serse.'

We were soon on our way, through the lanes that I was getting to know so well, having spent so much time on my bike cycling through them the past ten days. Before long we were in the hills – far away from where we should have been going to the town, until I recognised a sign for a village I'd heard of – Castellania.

'Castellania. This is where Coppi is from isn't it?' I asked in wonder.

'Yes it is, my boy. I have taken a small detour, I thought it was time to bring you up here finally, it is where the '*Il Campionissimo* story begins and ends,' he said as he pulled the pick up off the road leading up to the village, at a point which gave an excellent view of the small group of white bricked and red roofed houses that made up the village. The scene looked just like a small model village from this distance, all clustered as it was, tight together on the hilly mountainside.

'So, now you know that Fausto had a brother called Serse,' Grandpa started 'and Fausto loved him more than anything else on earth, they were very close. I think that the happiest I ever saw Fausto was on the day that he lost a race, even one as grueling as the Paris-Roubaix. Now, you remember I told you how awful riding in that great race was?' I nodded, 'and you know how much the desire for victory burned within Fausto every time that he sat on a bike?'

'Yes,' I nodded again

'Good, well that tells you all you need to know about how much he loved his brother Serse, for it was he that beat Fausto in the Hell of the North race of 1949, and Fausto simply couldn't have been happier.'

'So Serse was a pretty good cyclist then?' I asked.

'Oh yes, Danilo, he was much better than an old Gregario like me, but Serse had a problem. As talented a cyclist as he was, he had to deal with the fact that his brother was arguably the greatest cyclist who had ever sat on a bike. Professional cycling is hard enough at the best of times, so for Serse, it must have been extremely hard to live in that shadow every day as he tried to forge a career like the rest of us. It was easier for us because we knew what our job, and more importantly, our limitations were. We were the gregari, there to support and help our Patron as best we could – we had no other hopes apart from helping him deliver yet another victory for the team. But for Serse it was different, he was in a difficult position. He knew he wouldn't be as good as his brother, but he also knew he was better than us. Fausto understood his brother's dilemma completely, and that is why he tried at every turn to help his brother's career in any way that he could. That desire delivered to Serse the biggest victory of his career, winner in 1949 of the Hell of the North, but the circumstances of Fausto's assistance to his brother in this victory also put our Patron in a poor light with many, many people for probably the only time in his career.'

'The circumstances which delivered Serse victory in the race are still argued about today', he continued. 'I remember the day very well because, as usual in Paris at Easter, the weather was completely miserable when we all lined up at the start. The result of this heavy rain meant that the cobbles were as slick, slippery and dirty as I ever remember them. I shudder now thinking about it. There had been so much rain that pools of it just gathered and stood on the surface of the roads or 'pave'. This meant that not only did you run the risk of sliding off the cobbles as they were like ice, but also we had to cycle in a constant spray of muddy water, thrown up by the rear wheels of the bikes ahead of us. But there was another, hidden danger too. The standing water and puddles also hid many of the inevitable holes that existed in the road's surface from the missing cobbles. Hitting these at race speed resulted often in punctures and buckled wheels at best, or even accidents and broken bones at worst. The Hell of the North was the only time I spent on a bike when I believed it would be better for me to be back on the farm with my brother, I will admit that' said my grandfather with a rueful smile. 'By the time we approached the end of this race which finished inside Roubaix's packed velodrome, our beautiful blue and white jerseys were the colour of the soil in my fields in deepest winter, and our faces were hidden by the mud and muck of the roads of northern France. Anyway, that controversial year of 1949, as I came into the stadium, I could see over to the finish line on the other side where a sprint to the finish was just ending, in which Serse had done fantastically well not only to get himself involved in, but also to hold off everyone, including Fausto, to cross the line first.'

My grandfather then laughed before continuing: 'Well, that certainly would have been the case if they were not already presenting the Frenchman Andre Mahe with his winner's prize just as Serse was busy beating the others in his sprint.'

'How come ... I don't understand,' I said. 'You said he won the sprint?'

'He did – in a way! But what I haven't told you is that we had all been left behind by a three-man breakaway earlier in the day that Mahe had been part of. What we didn't know at the time was that when they got to the stadium, the three of them were greeted by chaos, such was the number of the crowds arriving at the velodrome trying to get inside in time to witness the finish. Not knowing exactly which way to go, Mahe and his companions asked a gendarme who, not being a race official, sent them the wrong way. Then, in the end, with all the panic and confusion that was facing them, they came into the stadium through the wrong entrance from the wrong route – a terrible error for a professional cyclist. But, this still meant that Mahe and his escapers were the first across the line in the velodrome, and so Mahe was awarded the victory by the judges. However, when Mahe's mix up outside the stadium was explained to us all, Fausto instantly instructed Serse to make an immediate appeal to all the judges for him and not Mahe, to be named as the winner of the race, disqualifying the three who had gone the wrong way. The facts you see were clear to us. In professional cycling, if you leave the planned route for any reason, and do not complete the course exactly, then there is only one outcome.'

'Disqualification?' I asked.

'Absolutely. This is a lesson you would do well to remember – always learn your route to the final centimetre when you race because if you get it wrong, and then get booted off the race, you will have nobody to blame but yourself. And that is exactly how we felt about Andre Mahe's predicament – he had nobody to blame but himself. So, that afternoon at the velodrome, Fausto used every influence he had earned in our sport to help deliver the victory to his brother, a victory that Fausto and us absolutely believed was Serse's by right. And that is what happened, with the judges agreeing with us. Mahe and the other two breakaway riders were disqualified and Serse was awarded the victory to the absolute and total delight of Fausto. I swear that he had displayed more enjoyment in witnessing his brother's victory that I ever saw him show for any of his own.'

I sat there and tried to understand what my grandfather had just told me and gave some thought to the outcome of the race for a moment and felt that it just didn't feel right somehow. I couldn't help but feel that Fausto had cheated Andre Mahe out of the win. 'I'm sorry Grandpa, I just don't think that's fair, it sounds to me that Serse only won because Fausto was his brother, and that's not right. I feel really sorry for the other bloke, Mahe. Serse only really came fourth.'

'Danilo, for a young boy, your sense of honour and judgement impresses me greatly, but there is still more to be told in this story, and also something else you must understand about a Champion which is an important thing for you to realise about the mind that a Champion possesses. I was once told a phrase by my English masseur Eddie which made me laugh so much, that I have never forgotten it. We were talking about what it takes to be a Champion, not just the talent or the hard to work, but that little bit extra that sets you apart. Anyway, Eddie said 'You must be willing to kick your own grandmother up the arse to get a victory', and I just burst out laughing. But he was right, most true champions in any sport must have that absolute, total and utter belief that they cannot be beaten – whatever the circumstances. It is called being ruthless I think? And this is exactly what Fausto had, ruthlessness more than any other Champion I witnessed in my career. So, when he went straight to the judges with Serse after he heard the true circumstance behind Andre Mahe's victory, he used the same determination, commitment and energy as he would have if he was still on his bike trying to win a race on the road. His belief in doing the right thing for his brother was total. And, as usual in those days, Fausto won. The judges heard all the arguments, made up their minds, and they disqualified Mahe and the others before awarding Serse the victory. It caused lots of controversy, and many people lost respect for Fausto that day, because they believed that he abused his position as champion, just to get his brother a win. I saw it all, and I don't believe that. I was one hundred per cent behind Fausto, one hundred per cent. We all knew that Mahe had gone the wrong way, simple as that, it was his responsibility to complete the exact course – not one hundred and sixty-four miles of the exact course and then a different half a mile to the rest of us. Therefore, beyond any argument, the first person to complete the exact course was Serse. This is what Fausto believed in his heart, and when he held that belief, he would, how can I say 'kick his own grandmother in the arse' to get the right result.'

I took in what my grandfather had said, and could see that he had a point. It seemed that I was going to have to grow up to be quite tough if I really wanted to succeed in my dream of becoming a pro cyclist. After a moment's thought, I spoke again. 'So what happened next, Grandpa?'

My grandfather sighed as he looked up at the small village on the hill. 'First, there were more troubles to come over Serse's victory, that took their toll on Fausto, with many people still pointing the finger at him, saying that Serse had only won because of him and that Andre should be awarded the race back. It went on for a long time, at one point the authorities took the race off both Serse and Andre and declared the race void with no winner, but months later a compromise was reached where they were both declared as joint winners, so the record books show that for the only time in history, the Paris-Roubaix had two winners. The whole affair lit a fire within Fausto. In one of our winter training runs later on, he told me that he would ensure that a Coppi, and a Coppi alone would be the winner's name the next year. And that is what happened. He left no stone unturned in his preparation for the race. He worked with the Bianchi mechanic to build a special bike more suited to the demands of the cobbles, than any built before. Then, unlike Andre Mahe, he studied the exact route that was laid down that year, including finding out where the best places to avoid the worst of the cobbles were, and take advantage of those stretches. Even his warm up was the most anyone had ever done – over thirty miles – before the race event started! All this meant that when he lined up at the start on those hated cobbles that year, I don't believe that any cyclist in history was better prepared for victory in that particular race. And let me tell you, it certainly paid off. Fausto dominated almost from the start and spent much of the race in a breakaway with the Frenchman Maurice Diot before dropping him with about thirty miles to go, with his final attack. Fausto arrived at the velodrome alone, resulting in him winning comfortably in front of a packed stadium and, most importantly, having followed the correct route. I don't think I ever saw him more determined to win a race, and I really believe he saw his victory as a matter of putting the Coppi family record straight, not just in terms of putting the family name back on the list of winners alone, but also silencing all of those who had doubted his intentions just a year before. Whatever it was, he had delivered on his promise, but on that day of unbridled joy and happiness, none of us – especially Serse and Fausto themselves – had any idea of the tragedy that awaited them both.'

27

AS we gazed out of my grandfather's pick-up at the quiet, peaceful village above us, my grandfather sat in silence for what seemed like an age before relating the chain of events that brought such sorrow to the Coppi family, a depth of sadness for which I wasn't prepared.

'The tragedy that affected Serse Coppi happened in June of 1951 at the Giro del Piemonte, an important race that Fausto never actually won,' he began. 'That day had been a particularly tough day because it was extremely hot, which can be very difficult for a cyclist. Anyway, we had been out on the roads all day when we finally made it to the last sprint to the line in which so much can happen. The trouble is, so many people take risks when they are travelling at the highest of speeds, and as a result, it can often be really dangerous. It is common for crashes to occur, but unless they involve you or happen right in front of you, it is normal that you pay no heed to them until you get told of the events, long after the race is finished.'

My grandfather paused, as he looked into the distance, troubled by the memory, before continuing.

'I was actually way back in the field that day and by the time I got to the line, I could see that there had been an incident because Serse was getting back onto his bike. He looked fine to me, and I didn't pay much attention to it because hardly a day passed by without somebody falling off somewhere. It was only later when we saw the ambulance arrive at the team hotel that we began to worry that it was something much worse. We were later told that Serse had started to receive terrible pain inside his head back at the hotel and after the ambulance had taken him to the hospital, he collapsed when they were treating him and he died there and then. He had suffered a brain haemorrhage, and like that, this beautiful young boy was gone. He was but twenty-eight years old with the whole of his life ahead for him to live. The devastation we felt was total, but even this did not compare to Fausto's grief. He was never the same man again.'

There was so much I wanted to ask my grandfather about the incident, but he was still clearly upset by the memory of it, so I stayed silent and let him continue when he was ready.

'Just five days after poor Serse was buried on that hill up there,' said my solemn grandfather pointing up to the village, 'The 1951 Tour de France began. Fausto had said immediately that he would not enter but even more than that, he would retire from cycling straight away in respect of his brother's memory. It was terrible. It was the only time in my life, whether for good or for bad, that I didn't know what was the right thing to do. I am only glad that I was not faced with such a choice. Serse was everything to Fausto and I think that up to that point of his career, Fausto saw part of his reason for cycling as being an instructor and teacher to his brother for him to eventually become the Patron after his career finished. Now, with Serse not alive to fulfil that hope, he saw no point in carrying on.'

'Did he quit, Grandpa?' I asked.

'Very, very nearly. His wife and family begged him to, as I'm sure did many others. But what he did instead was embark on the bravest and most impressive tribute that these old eyes have ever witnessed. He decided at the very last moment to take part in the Tour. I think that part of the reason was out of loyalty to his sponsors and the organisers of the race, and of course to the tifosi, the fans who adored him. But the real reason was Serse. He wanted to do something that would ensure his brother's memory was secure. So instead, Fausto tortured himself, and did it in memory of his beloved young brother.'

'Tortured himself?'

'Let me explain. Hopefully Danilo, you will one day understand what it is to become a cyclist, I know that this is your dream. But there is one quality you must have in order to undertake what is so often an extremely brutal existence. I have mentioned to you the fitness, the nutrition and the commitment that are all required to face these challenges, but above all there is this,' and my grandfather tapped the right temple on the side of his head with his thick index finger.

'The mind. If you are not in the right frame of mind, if you do not believe that what you are about to do is achievable, then in a race as brutal as the Tour de France, you only invite one sensation – torture – and that is exactly what Fausto endured for the first nineteen days of the Tour de France – 2,305 miles of tourture.' My grandfather closed his eyes, bowed his head and shook it slowly, as if he was experiencing pain himself.

He continued: 'We knew within the first hour of the race that Fausto simply should not have been there. He was a shell of the man that we knew him to be. He was so devastated by the death of Serse, that he had nothing mentally to give in the race that demands absolutely everything you have. I have mentioned several times that Fausto was a great Champion, yes?' my grandfather nodded at me,

'Yes, of course,' I replied.

'Well one thought a Champion needs to drive him on is the knowledge that he has a chance to win. I have ridden with many men who liked to think that they were Champions, but when the chance of victory was removed, by a puncture or a crash, then I have seen them just step off the bike and quit. There were many times in the first nineteen days of that Tour that I prayed Fausto would do just that, get off and quit, but he didn't. It was as though the more pain and torture he put himself through, the more respect he was paying to his beloved brother Serse. One day in particular was more pathetic than the rest. It was the stage into Montpellier from Carcassonne, Stage 16, one hundred and thirteen miles through the Pyrenees, a very tough stage. It was won by the eventual winner of the Tour that year, Hugo Koblet, but none of us saw that victory, we were all at the very back of the field, surrounding Fausto, staying with him and supporting him for as long as he needed us. Our job was quite simple usually – do everything in our power to deliver Fausto to the front of the race, and then bask in the reflected glory of another victory by our Patron. But this was so much different. We could only ride with him and hope that our presence alongside would somehow deliver him enough strength to carry on. In every stage of the Tour de France, the riders at the back of the race have to finish within a certain time of the winner, if not, you were out – eliminated. That day into Montpellier was the closest that the great Fausto came to this indignity. The very fact that it didn't happen was purely down to the amount of suffering that man could endure, such was his mental state. But amazingly, rather than the fans turn against Fausto for what many could perceive to be a disappointing performance, the love and respect for him grew to even greater heights due to his total refusal to give in and walk away, and mourn in grief, the loss of his beautiful brother. He had no chance of winning the Tour, and he had made his point in his painful tribute to the brother he loved, but yet he kept going day after horrible day. Many feel that this was his greatest Tour, for certainly it was his bravest.

'So what happened?' I asked. 'Did he just finish last every day?'

'Almost Danilo, almost. But then, prior to Stage 20, he addressed us all quietly one morning before we pedalled to the start line in Gap, which was the toughest and highest mountain stage of that year's Tour, up through the Alps into Briancon. With no fuss, Fausto spoke and said that the suffering was over, he thanked us all for our loyalty in supporting him through his pain, but that now was the time to deliver a victory for Serse. And that was it, he said no more. He treated that stage as his personal tribute to Serse, and despite all the pain and suffering he had inflicted on himself in those previous nineteen days, he still had the strength of mind to be able to pull out the performance of a Champion and totally destroy a world class field by winning that immense stage through the Alps to Briancon, by almost four minutes from the next man. It was truly astonishing.'

'A light went out within Fausto that year with the loss of Serse, and despite other victories that still came, I don't believe Fausto was ever the same man again.'

28

WE sat in my grandfather's pick-up for a while, silent, both of us with our thoughts, me considering just what a massive influence on my grandfather's life had been this time living alongside *Il Campionissimo*, and my grandfather lost, no doubt, in the ghosts and memories of his past. As we sat there in silence, I began to understand how amazing it must have been for just a normal farming man like my grandfather, to come to terms much later in his life, with the fact that he shared his best years, the years of his youth, with a man who came to be regarded as a sporting legend. I understood that he was only too aware of how unique the experience was, and how very lucky he had been, to have witnessed the life of this national superstar first hand. I also began to understand the main reason behind why my grandfather had treated my father in the truly awful way that he had. He knew how important it was that he passed on all the lessons, all the examples of sportsmanship he had learned at the side of Coppi, to somebody who could use them, somebody who themselves may have had a future as a cyclist. That person was my dad. Sadly, as it turned out, my grandfather simply didn't have the skills to deliver those lessons in the correct way. But now, after learning from the mistakes he'd made with my dad, he certainly did. I think my grandfather had seen it as his duty to make sure that someone he had influence over would keep alive everything that Fausto Coppi stood for – his elegance, his talent, his determination, his honour and his pride. But most of all, his spirit. He had blown that chance with his own son, succeeding only in pushing him as far away as humanly possible from the dreams he must have had for him, and Coppi's memory. He must have spent the previous twenty years kicking himself every day for destroying a talent that had as much chance as anyone of succeeding the incredible Coppi as a champion. Did he now think that I was the one to deliver on his dream? Did he seriously think that I could be Coppi? Maybe I could be, I loved everything I'd heard about the man, was certainly inspired by him and decided I wanted to base my career on him if I did make it as a professional. After some more thought, I spoke. In retrospect, what I asked, was rather a stupid question.

'Grandpa, do you think I could be a Coppi?'

He stared straight ahead, not even looking at me as he answered. 'No,' he said, bluntly.

I was really disappointed. What was the point of him telling me all this stuff about Coppi if he didn't think I could be as good as him? I must admit I was really hoping he would have said yes. I tried not to show how disappointed I was by his reply.

'Danilo, I know from your silence that I have disappointed you and I am sorry. But I believed long ago that one such as you could be Coppi, and look what I did. I totally ruined your father, because it was he that I held this dream for. It took me many years to understand, that it is wrong to try to recreate somebody in the body of someone else, especially when that man was as remarkable a man as Fausto Coppi. So, no, I do not think that you can be him ... nobody can.'

He paused for a moment before carrying on, 'But, what I do believe in my heart, is that if you have listened to these stories and if you have recognised something within them that will be of benefit to you in your life – whether or not that life includes cycling or not, then I believe that has been far, far more important to you than if I had just taught you how to win a cycling race.'

'Wherever your life takes you, whether you end up working in a bank or for the council, you must use all the knowledge and all the stories I have told you about Fausto to help you to achieve the one success above others that he managed to accomplish fully...'

'Be the best that I can be,' I said sincerely before he had chance of finishing.

'Exactly. That is all I ask of you as your grandfather. Be the best that you can be. When I look back now, I have come to realise that is all Fausto did. It's just that I didn't understand that his best was way better than anyone else who had ever ridden a bike before. Regrettably, I judged people against Fausto and believed that those who never came up to his mark were failures – myself included. Oh how wrong I was. The key – for all of us – is to be the best that you can be. So please, whatever you chose to do in life, just do it well, do it with all your heart and soul, and then you yourself – the only person who will ever really know how hard you have tried – can be a contented man.'

I looked at this old man as he stared at me, almost willing me to understand him and absorb the message he was giving me. He needn't have worried. 'I understand now,' I said, 'and I understand why you have told me all these stories about Coppi.'

'Good, I am pleased,' he said, ruffling my hair. 'Come on, we have been much longer than I thought, we'd better go and get your grandmother's shopping,' and he started the engine. As he did, I spoke: 'But I promise you now Grandpa, as we look at the slopes of the village on which Coppi was born and lived, I will be the best I can be, but it won't be in a bank or for a council. I will be the best I can be on a bike, and I will come back here and show you that. And I will use the knowledge of Fausto Coppi to make good on that promise. But I have one favour to ask of you Grandpa.'

'Certainly my boy, anything you ask. What is this favour?'

'That you will stick around and see it.'

My grandfather laughed, held out his hand, spat on it and said: 'That is a deal.'

We shook on it there and then, and as we drove away from Coppi's village, I knew, right at that moment, that I had found my purpose in life. This was not some childish schoolboy promise, this was it. This was my promise, my solemn oath to myself, to my grandfather and most importantly I also realised, to the spirit of Fausto Coppi.

I was going to be the best I could be, and I was going to come back here, to these very roads, and prove it to my grandfather, one day, in the greatest Italian race of all. I knew that now.

29

ON the final day of my holiday, my father, grandfather and I made a pilgrimage back to Castellania. But only the outskirts, Grandpa wouldn't go further. By now I had been told of the sad, tragic end to Coppi's life, where he died a horribly painful death, misdiagnosed by some arrogant doctors who dismissed the advice that *Il Campionissimo* was suffering from malaria. Instead they treated him for some form of influenza, when a simple injection of quinine would have saved his life. He was dead, aged just forty, and a nation mourned, united in grief.

When my grandfather had told me about the circumstances of Coppi's death, my father and I just sat in total silence, trying to absorb it all. Even though my dad had heard it before and I had already suspected that Coppi had died young, I still found the circumstances of his death quite shocking. It was clear from what my grandfather said, that he could and should, have been saved. Coppi was one of several leading cyclists invited to a race in Burkina Faso, then known as Upper Volta in Africa, where the plan was that they would take part in a local race, get treated like Kings while they were there, experience the unique sights that Africa offers and get paid handsomely for doing it. A dream trip really. But the dream turned into a nightmare. Apparently, the accommodation that Coppi and the French cyclist who had organised the trip, Raphael Geminiani, were allocated on the game reserve was infested with mosquitoes. Coppi, who had suffered with malaria earlier in life from his time in a prisoner of war camp in Africa, was to contract the illness again. This time, it would be fatal.

Three weeks after returning from the ill fated trip, both Coppi and Geminiani were extremely sick in hospital. The grave misfortune for Coppi was that they were in different hospitals. In France, the fortunate Geminiani was given many different tests to find out the cause of the illness that was killing him. Eventually it was found to be malaria. The type of malaria that he was diagnosed with was one of the most deadly types, bringing death within ten days if not treated. As soon as Geminiani was diagnosed and treated with the drug quinine, which provided an almost instant cure, his wife rang Coppi's doctors and told them how they should treat Coppi. Astonishingly, the doctors ignored her and refused to alter their treatment. They insisted it was not malaria. Within nine days, Geminiani was up and about and getting back to full health. In the same time span, Coppi was dead. As he told us this, my grandfather was even angrier than the time when he had told me about the Germans who had killed his father, so angry in fact that he was certain that the doctors had murdered Coppi 'as sure as if they had put a gun to his head and pulled the trigger.' I must admit, hearing this story 40 odd years later, I too was filled with anger. If those inept doctors had just listened to the wife of Geminiani or just talked to the doctors at her husband's hospital in France, then Coppi would have been saved. There is no doubt about that. The more I thought about it, the more I agreed with my grandfather, that not to take these steps and check the facts out was nothing short of criminal. But I was sorry for another reason too. I realised that the death of Coppi had in many ways, altered my grandfather's life forever. He became completely and utterly lost after Coppi's death, and totally withdrew into himself and life on his farm. Apart from his family, he cut himself off from everyone for years. Coppi's passing came in the year that Grandpa had to retire from cycling due to his injuries, so at more or less the same time he lost both his youthful and active life along with his best friend, almost overnight. But, far more importantly, the absence of Coppi in my grandfather's life as he began to bring up his own son, meant that he subconsciously attempted – with disastrous results – to somehow bring back Coppi from the dead by recreating him in his own son. That was the direct consequence to my family of the criminal mistakes made by those doctors who let Coppi die on 2nd January 1960. My grandfather lost the most important figure in his life that day, and for the next forty-two years, until this holiday began three weeks ago, he had been wandering through his life, drifting without any purpose, apart from regretting the hurt he had caused his only son, in trying to resurrect a legend. It was as if Coppi's tragic early death was still causing problems for those closest to him over forty years on.

I decided that all the sorrow and regret had to end now. We all had to move on. I had an idea.

'I want to go to his grave,' I said. 'I want to lay flowers, and I want to thank him for the inspiration he has given me, through you Grandpa, you and the wonderful memories you have of him.'

My grandfather became a little choked at this suggestion, and waved his arm as if to say no.

My father spoke instead.

'Papa, I know I said the other day that what has happened in the past must remain in the past, but Danilo is right. For good and for bad, Fausto Coppi still hangs over you, both as a blessing and a curse. The curse was how the memory of him and your desire for him somehow to remain alive, ruined my love for you and nearly destroyed my life with my son. Papa, you must understand that indirectly, Coppi drove me away and caused such pain. However, the blessing we must never forget is the celebration of the wonderful life you lived and experienced with him, at the side of the finest sportsman that the whole of Italy has ever produced in its long, proud history. That is unique and should be remembered forever. It is just the negative side that should be put to the past forever. And we can do that, the three of us side by side at his grave, we will banish forever the pain that Coppi indirectly caused you and me, but also celebrate the inspiration he has given – and will continue to give Danilo. Then we can all move on, with forgiveness and hope in all our hearts.'

My grandfather was filled with emotion when he finally spoke.

'Luca, I have not been inside Castellania since the day that
Fausto was buried that cold January day. There were over 30,000
souls crammed into that tiny village, throughout each of its narrow
streets, from all over Italy and Europe to say farewell to *Il
Campionissimo*. I remember every solemn moment of that day, the
tears of his mother and the wonderful reading given by his old adver-
sary Gino Bartali, a man that once saw Fausto as his sworn enemy,
but who grew to respect and love Fausto like the rest of us. It will be
very hard for me to visit there after such a long time, but,' he paused
for several moments, 'I suppose, with you and my beautiful grandson
at my side, I will have the strength.' He paused again. 'You are both
right of course, it is time to lay the past to rest and look to the future.
The future of the first Danilo Rossi, not the next Fausto Coppi.

This time, we drove into the village, the tiny village that was the
birthplace to two fine sportsmen and brothers, who were now joined
again, side by side, in a memorial to them both, in the heart of the
village. We parked alongside, and walked into the memorial.

The three of us stood there, in front of the beautiful monument
to both Fausto and Serse Coppi, saying little, but just letting go of
the demons of the past, but also paying due and grateful respect to
the everlasting achievements of *Il Campionissimo*.

I looked at the graves and memorials to these two brothers who
lived for cycling, but who both, tragically, lost their lives because of
it. In front of the two memorials, and standing between them both,
was a beautiful bronze bust of Fausto. I looked into the lifeless eyes
of this striking sculpture, and thought back to all the stories my
grandfather had told me about this handsome man, about his sense
of honour, commitment, excellence and fair play. If I didn't know
already, I knew at that exact moment as I looked at his statuesque
sculpture, exactly what I was going to devote the rest of my life to.
Cycling. No question. No quitting.

Then, for no obvious reason, I started to cry. And when I started,
I just couldn't stop. My grandfather held me for what seemed an eter-
nity. I think everything I'd experienced in this amazingly powerful

three weeks poured out of me there and then; my initial disappointment of having to come to Italy in the first place; the horrible way I behaved and treated my father; the day of reckoning between my father and his own father; the inspirational stories of Fausto's many victories; the tragic stories of the deaths of the Coppi brothers. The emotion needed to come out, and come out it did, in torrents.

When it was over, and my wonderful grandfather had dried my tears and cleaned my face, I walked forward to the two memorials to these fine and gifted sportsmen and laid the flowers we had bought from a shop in the village in between the many other floral tributes that already had been laid for these outstanding, tragic cyclists. Before I moved away and re-joined my father and grandfather who were chatting closely as they made their way back to the wagon, I leant forward and gently touched the face of the bust of Fausto Coppi, this man who, via the stories of his gregario – my grandfather – had now become the central hero and inspiration in my life. The man I would now devote every available moment in my life, until I achieved my goal, to become a professional cyclist and come back to Italy and compete in the great races that Coppi won. As my fingers felt the cold roughness of the metal, as they touched his face on the beautiful bronze bust I quietly whispered: 'I will be back Patron, and I will win.'

Epilogue
Milan, Italy. Spring 2017

SO that was it, despite a few more days of cycling with Dad and Grandpa and many more tales about Coppi's great victories, a change had already occurred within me and was now cast in stone, there was no going back on it. Three weeks in Italy all those years years ago, and without that small, almost insignificant period of time in my life, I simply would not be in this small hotel room today, waiting, hoping and praying that tomorrow brings me the victory I crave, in the Milan – San Remo. Wow, The Milan – San Remo? I can still hardly believe that I am here. Only my fifth full classic race in my career, after four years first following my Olympic cycling dream, and then the last six years as a professional, but missing so many of these important races due to my many injuries.

'Be the best that you can be – that is all anyone can ever ask of you Danilo, nothing more my boy.' I hear the voice of my grandfather every day, and those words are as true now as they were when I was a little spoilt kid, meeting him for the first time all those years ago.

I have again remembered the innocent love and passion for

cycling that I first learned in this country, and tomorrow – if nothing else – I will be the best that I can be, riding with the spirit of Fausto Coppi inside me, and the love of my father and grandfather all around me.

The best that I can be. I can manage that, I always do. But will it be enough?

Race report of the 2017 Milan-San Remo
from *The International Cycling Times* – 19th March 2017

ASTONISHING SCENES AT MILAN–SAN REMO
AS ROOKIE DOMINATES

It's the pick of the classics. The Milan-San Remo is the first – and longest – classic of the professional cycling season, but can sometimes become a procession which plays into the hands of the sprinters, especially if they can manage to cope with the late climbs of the Cipressa and Poggio. But this year was different, spectacularly different.

It was different because this year, the rug was surprisingly pulled from under the sprinter's wheels thanks to a break by the unheralded Welsh rider, Daniel Williams, who took the race by the scruff of the neck almost from the start. Cycling for the under pressure and cash strapped Team MotoStep, 28-year-old Williams made a solitary break just 35 kilometres out of Milan, in the full knowledge that race success from there meant staying away from the field for over 260 kilometres, or put another way, five hours. Some said his chances for ultimate success would be extremely unlikely at best. Most said it was racing suicide.

But, break he did, and with no word coming from his usually extrovert Team Director, Jacques Deschamps, as to whether he was following team orders or acting alone, Williams was ignored by the bunch, who – not unreasonably – considered it would be a matter of time before he was caught. Ignoring him was their first mistake.

In fairness to the strategists of the other teams, who grew more anxious the longer the Welshman stayed away, Williams is quite an easy man to ignore. In just his second season with the under achieving Team MotoStep, and with a promising youth career almost wrecked by a succession of devastating injuries and now long in the memories of the dim and distant past, Williams' increasingly uncer-

tain future within the struggling team gave new depth to the phrase 'Last Chance Saloon.'

Today, however, somebody somewhere had managed to light a fire under Williams' saddle because by the time he reached the foot of the Passo del Turchino, he had managed to stretch his lead to 35 minutes, quite a feat in the first 98 miles of racing. Informed opinion had it that this climb would see that time advantage being shrunk significantly by the peloton, now cycling with an urgency delivered by the grim realisation that they might have let the rabbit get too far ahead.

But all was not lost for the favourites now working hard to catch the startled rabbit. Importantly, they will have all known that it is not unheard of for an unknown rider like Williams to use a high profile race such as 'La Primavera' to try to put his stamp on a race with an eye catching break that would please his team's sponsors. They would have also known, too, that at some point, breaks like these – almost always doomed to failure from the start – would be snuffed out on one hill or other, the closer the race got to San Remo. Surely the Turchino would be the very hill where the snuffing would begin.

But as he had shown all day, Williams was nothing if not incredibly determined. A solid if unspectacular climber, the 28-year-old from Swansea showed fantastic technique as he flew up the slopes of the Turchino in the style reminiscent of an Indurain or a Pantani. But, for the older members of the crowd, viewing with great surprise the continued excellence of his riding, one other long forgotten name was being whispered. Fausto Coppi. Praise indeed.

In fact, as Williams emerged from the Turchino tunnel with such an advantage over the field, one or two local veteran spectators said that they had seen nothing like it since 1946 when 'Il Campionissimo' destroyed and humiliated fellow Italian legend Gino Bartali, who had mistakenly allowed Coppi to build up a similar lead to the one that Williams enjoyed as he emerged from that iconic cycling location yesterday.

However, the key difference between cycling today compared to the golden days of Coppi and Bartali is that old fashioned spirit and endeavour has been replaced by cold organisation and communication. As word filtered back to the team radios, informing the Racing Directors that Williams had succeeded in keeping his lead intact on the slopes of the Turchino, the cyclists' earpieces went into meltdown as they processed the renewed tactical orders of their Directors. These key strategists had now worked out exactly the pace required to catch Williams by the outskirts of San Remo. So, as the teams descended the slopes of the Turchino, the mother and father of all chasedowns began.

Whilst panic is not a word professional cyclists will thank you for using, pre race favourite and sprinter extraordinaire, Mark Cavendish, sitting behind Steve Cummings and the rest of the Dimension Data team, certainly wore the look of a concerned man as his team set about hauling back in the tiring Williams over the final key couple of climbs of the day.

The pace now adopted by Dimension Data effectively shattered the peloton, resulting in some men who would have harboured hopes of success in San Remo being unceremoniously shot out the back of an exploding bunch. The only team that were able to withstand the unrelenting onslaught of Cavendish's team was Team Sky, containing one of the pre race favourites Michal Kwiatkowski and Britain's Ian Stannard, who even managed to share the work at the front with Cavendish's men. But even with this huge increase of effort, all concerned must have doubted whether it would be enough to catch the leader Williams.

By the time that Williams reached the last 10 kilometres on the outskirts of San Remo, his previously unassailable lead of 35 minutes was down to just five, as the relentless pursuit of Dimension Data and Sky continued. But the added ingredient to that statistic was that Williams, to coin a phrase, had blown up. Surely his race was run and it would be a matter of time – literally – before he was caught. Nevertheless, the crowd were delirious as they cheered the heroic effort of the now almost totally spent Welshman, despite his lead continuing to evaporate with each turn of his pedals as he painfully struggled on.

As he passed under the red kite mark which marked one kilometre to the finish, his lead was just 34 seconds, and the pain Williams was enduring, pointed to him being caught comfortably before the line. But, with just 100 metres to go, Williams swept round the final bend, and managed to summon one final effort which saw him out of the saddle, weaving insanely with his efforts to get to the line. But, it was also the moment that Dimension Data launched Cavendish, the world's fastest sprinter, to finally seize his prey. With 75 metres to go, Williams led Cavendish by 30. With 50 to go, his lead was just 20. Then, with 10 to go, it was down to a couple of bike lengths. From somewhere, as Cavendish pounced, Williams found energy for a final, painful surge which ensured that the front wheels of both Cavendish and him crossed the line together in a blur.

There was no usual victory salute from Cavendish as he swerved violently to narrowly avoid smashing into the group of press photographers, clumped together on the left of the course, but instead the crowd gasped as an unconscious Williams crashed into the safety barriers on the right hand side, just yards after crossing the line in obvious distress. The hysteria of the crowd instantly turned to silence as the seriousness of Williams condition became apparent. Big Screen television replays showed Williams' hands actually coming off the handlebars prior to crossing the line, marking his descent into exhaustion induced unconsciousness, before his rudderless bike veered at right angles, straight into the crash barriers at the side of the finish line. The screams of the crowds as they relived this moment on the screen revealed the sickening impact his head and face had on the barriers. The descent into silence of the thousands present at the finishing line, showed the genuine fear the people had about his fate. Paramedics were instantly on scene and attending to the apparently seriously injured rider.

However, in addition to the serious medical concerns over Williams, the outcome of the race was still unclear. Initially, an official announcement was made that both cyclists were being given the same time, but that decision was thrown into instant confusion by a further public announcement stating that it was the decision of the Director of the race that the timing should go down to a thousandth of a second, not the hundredth of a second that was usually used to split the cyclists.

After over 10 minutes of deliberations, a further announcement informed the massed crowds, and thankfully, the now conscious but bloodied Williams sitting at the side of the road, refusing a neck brace that was offered him, that the Race Director's decision was final, and Cavendish was awarded the race by 3 thousandths of a second, which, over a distance of 298 kilometres was about the width of half a matchstick.

The crowd's reaction to the announcement said it all. Boos rang around the throng of supporters, which soon turned to applause as the defeated Williams was finally helped to his feet and away to the team caravan by his father and team doctor, his face, jersey and arms smeared with his crimson blood.

But Williams' exit was merely a prelude to even more drama in a race that had already provided so much. Cavendish, known throughout the peloton as a straight talker and a man of emotion and impulse was seen to be in a furious public argument with the race organisers prior to his arrival at the winner's podium to accept his victory award. The reason for his passionate discussion soon became clear.

The cheers that greeted the wounded Williams at the podium, looking remarkably composed despite sporting a broken nose, a gash above his right eye and a missing front tooth from his crash, bordered on hysteria as he was handed his prize for a courageous second place. But, no sooner had the cheers died down, Cavendish displayed one of the finest pieces of sportsmanship this reporter has seen in over 25 years of covering professional cycling.

As the honourable Mayor of San Remo stepped forward with the iconic winners trophy for Cavendish, so the great sprinter attempted to drag Williams onto the top step to share the winners spoils. Williams protested instantly and was seen to clearly and vigorously say to the gracious Cavendish, 'No, I did my best, but I wasn't good enough – you won fair, it's yours.'

Undaunted, Cavendish, understanding that Williams' pride would not allow him to move to the top step of the podium, made the amazing gesture of stepping down onto the runners-up spot and refusing the trophy.

The cheers that greeted this were even louder than those for Williams just moments earlier, which soon turned to laughter as the honourable Mayor stood abandoned on the podium, clutching the trophy, but with no idea what to do with it.

It took legendary champion, and seven time Milan – San Remo winner, Eddie Merckx in his capacity of Chief Representative of the race sponsors to sort the situation out. He mounted the podium, took the trophy from a bemused Mayor and spoke to the crowd:

'Ladies and Gentlemen, today we have witnessed true sporting greatness. A young man making the bravest of breakaways caught on the line by a sprinter who is the best in the world. However, Cavendish has shown that cycling is about more than just winning and losing, especially when that margin can only be proved by a computer. So, I believe I am correct in announcing that unless the race victory is shared, Mark Cavendish is refusing to be named winner?'

Extraordinarily, Cavendish nodded, and the crowd erupted as both men now took the top step to jointly receive the spoils of victory in such an important race. An extraordinary sporting moment in an extraordinary sporting day. But one final, incredible, surprise remained.

Prior to the official presentation of the trophy, on a day of such unpredictability, the partisan Italian crowd who pray for nothing less than an Italian winner each year, bizarrely got their reward. Merckx, ignoring the now totally bewildered Mayor, called 89-year-old Umberto Rossi out of the crowd to make the final presentation. To the unbridled delight of everyone, Rossi was not only identified by Merckx as the former team-mate of Fausto Coppi in the legendary all conquering Bianchi team of the 1950s, but also – unknown to anyone in and around the peloton – as the grandfather of Daniel Williams. The joyous Italians now had their Italian winner, or perhaps more accurately Italian-Welsh joint-winner. The sight of this proud old cyclist greeting both his grandson and Cavendish so warmly was a truly touching moment, leaving even the most cynical, hard nosed sports writers in the crowd nodding happily in recognition of a just and fair outcome of this enormously eventful Milan-San Remo.

Fittingly, the final words went to the no longer unknown Williams. When questioned on the podium by Merkx about where he had found the energy to stay out on his own for so long, yet still managing to summon enough strength to match Cavendish's surge for the line, he said simply and modestly, 'From my grandfather'. The crowd cheered uncontrollably.

Merckx stated that his grandfather was clearly a big influence on him, Williams smiled, nodded and continued, 'Yes, absolutely. Growing up, I was taught on these very roads by my grandfather about the spirit of Fausto Coppi and how he never gave in no matter what pain he was in. More importantly though, I also learned that despite all Coppi's wins and achievements, every day, all he ever tried to do was the very same thing – and that was to be the best that he could be. Throughout all the many disappointments in my sporting life – and there have been many – that's all I've ever tried to do, even if I ended up coming last, it was the best I could do that day. I figured out long ago, that if trying to be the best that you could be worked for Fausto, then it would hopefully, one day, work for me, and today was that day. Since my grandfather taught me about him, Coppi has always been the cyclist I've tried to follow most. Today has proved that to be a very good decision, I could not have wished for a better cyclist to try to become ... after all, he will always be Il Campionissimo ...

... 'The Champion of Champions."

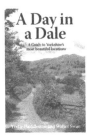

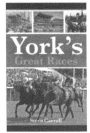

Investigate our other titles and
stay up to date with all our latest releases at
www.scratchingshedpublishing.co.uk